CRYSTALS, CROOKS, AND CHAOS

EMERALD CITY PARANORMAL COZY MYSTERY

THERESA CRATER

Crystals, Crooks, and Chaos

Emerald City Paranormal Cozy Mysteries

Copyright © 2025

Theresa Crater

Print ISBN: 979-8-9927156-5-1

Cover by Karri Klawiter

Crystal Star Publishing

www.crystalstarpublishing.com

 Formatted with Vellum

CONTENTS

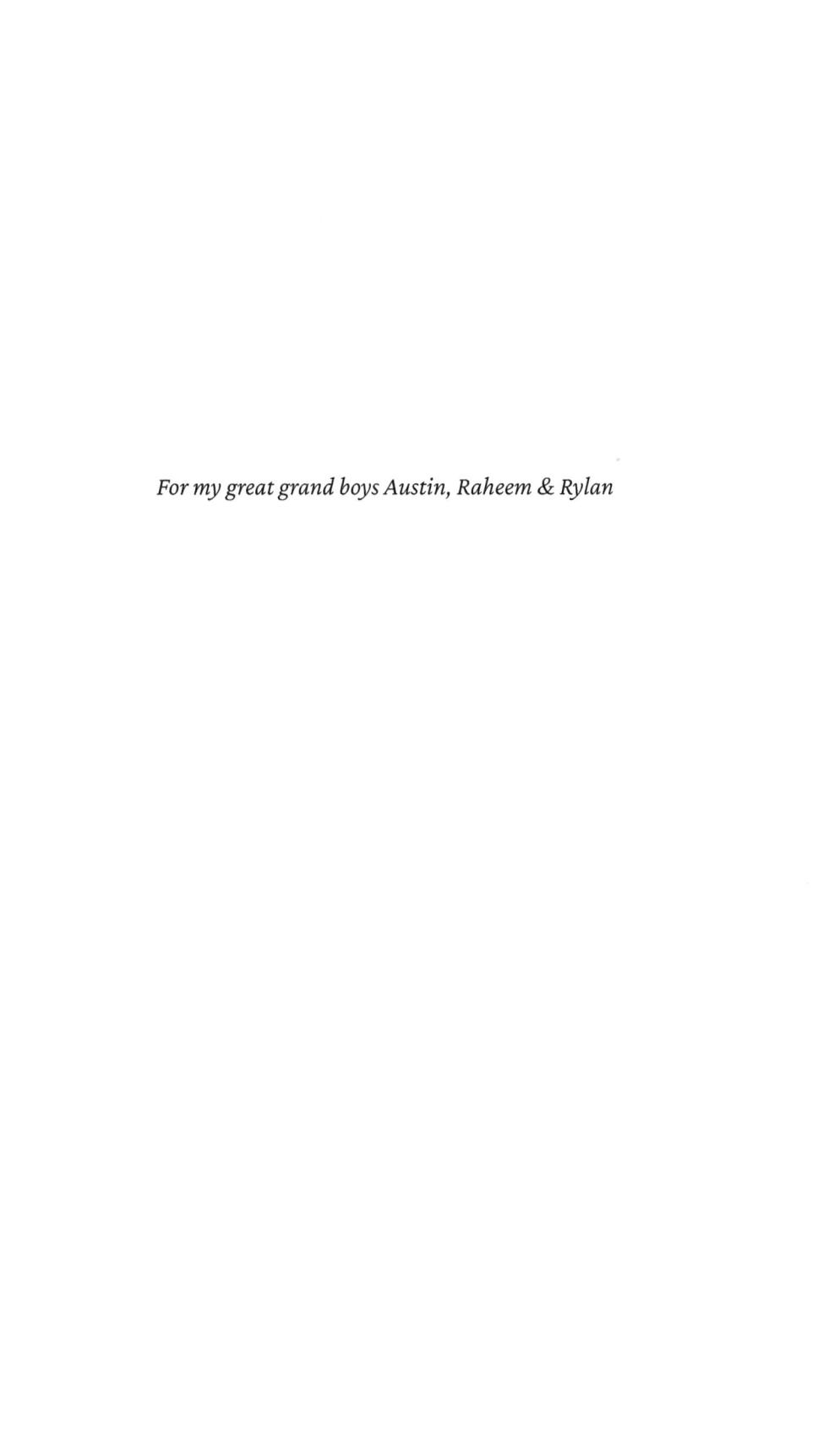

For my great grand boys Austin, Raheem & Rylan

CHAPTER
ONE

The Yule season was in full swing at Star, Stone & Flower. The scent of pine, frankincense, and warm beeswax candles curled through the air, wrapping the shop in a fragrant embrace. Outside, the slate sky pressed low over Seattle, but within these walls, golden light poured through frosted front windows and glinted off shelves crammed with glittering crystals, amber bottles of herbal tinctures, and hand-bound grimoires with curling leather edges.

The store hummed with life. And chaos. Midlife women in velvet coats and chunky scarves leaned over altars of sparkling necklaces, lifting each one to the light to watch it flare. Others uncapped tiny jars of wintergreen balm, the sharp scent mingling with the resinous incense that smoldered at the counter. A pair debated in low, conspiratorial tones over which dream-interpretation book held the *real* meaning behind a snowy owl sighting.

Near the pendulum display, a teenager with half her hair dyed ocean blue dangled a quartz sphere over her palm. "How do I find out if my ex is coming back?" she asked the universe—or perhaps the nearest patient-looking stranger.

At the back, a woman stood before a tray of amethyst points. One by one, she lifted each crystal to her third eye with quiet reverence, as though the right one might whisper its name.

Skye Yarrow drifted between customers like a current—offering gentle nudges of guidance, a flash of humor when needed, and the occasional raised eyebrow at those who needed it.

Thistle, the silver and gray sentinel of the shop, lounged high on a shelf, his tail twitching in slow arcs. Every so often, he fixed his sharp green gaze on some corner of the room, signaling to Skye in that unprovable way cats had. At least, she liked to think so. Laurie had never confirmed it.

He and his sister had appeared just past fall equinox, half-grown and thin as shadows, slipping inside to escape the damp autumn chill. Three months of good meals and warm hearths later, they were plump, sleek, and unrepentantly bossy.

The back buzzer startled her from her thoughts. Likely a late shipment, delayed by customs or holiday chaos. Skye caught her younger cousin Cillian's eye and tipped her head toward the swelling line at the front register. He gave her a brisk thumbs-up.

Slipping behind the swirled curtain to the shop's inner sanctum, she left the bustle behind. The space—usually for readings and private sessions—was now a temporary staging ground for Yule's flood of merchandise. Pagans loved Yule as much as Christians loved Christmas, and everybody bought gifts for family and friends. The tables bore neat drifts of tissue paper, coils of twine, and boxes half-emptied of their treasures.

Classes were paused for the season, but readings still drew the faithful. Luna sat at a corner table, her cards spread like a jeweled fan before a young woman with a dragon tattoo climbing one arm. The warm murmur of their voices was a comforting hum in the background.

The buzzer blared again.

Skye ducked through the back door into the storage area where a new UPS driver, cheeks raw from the cold, balanced a large box on one hip.

"Oh, there you are," he said, relief softening his voice. "This one needs a signature."

"Don't know what's coming this late," she said as she signed at the bottom of the form without giving it too much scrutiny. She didn't want to keep him standing in the cold.

Customers from the Midwest often teased that Seattle's mild winters were enviable—until they stepped into the damp chill that slid into one's bones. The air today sat on the edge of freezing, rain so thick it was flirting with sleet. Skye silently thanked the gods for coffee, the city's unofficial survival tool. Maybe she should expand, open a cafe if the salon next door went out of business.

She hefted the box and instantly regretted it. It was bulky, awkward, and heavier than she expected. Inch by inch, she wrestled it inside, hitting the buzzer for help.

Sorcha answered in her clipped, singsong way. "Yeah?"

"I need some help with a delivery."

"I'll send Cillian," came the reply, then, with a wheedle, "When can I do some tarot readings?"

"After the Yule rush," Skye said firmly. "Learning to run the front end is important, too."

The sigh on the other end was theatrical enough to earn a smile. Sorcha might be a gifted seer, but at Star, Stone & Flower, everyone learned the ropes.

Cillian arrived and between the two of them they managed to squeeze the bulky box through the 'Employees Only' door onto the long table set up for unpacking. Skye sliced open the tape with a practiced flick of the box cutter, revealing a drift of compostable peanuts. Thank the powers that more people were using them.

"Oh, good. Here's more incense." Skye pulled out a container of sandalwood. "And here's some rose. All the scents we use. Let's get these out on the shelves."

Cillian gathered an armful and vanished through the curtain.

Skye dug deeper, unearthing incense burners shaped like spirals of smoke and whimsical sun catchers—one with Santa and his elves, another a dancing spiral of reindeer and sleigh.

Then her fingers touched something hard, square, and unyielding. It sat at the bottom, encased in layers of Styrofoam. Skye's nose wrinkled at the sight. This stuff would outlive humanity itself.

She turned the square over, curiosity prickling. It was sealed tight, as though someone had gone to great lengths to keep it safe—or hidden. The tape resisted, but at last the top half came free.

A dome of crystal gleamed in the overhead light.

She caught her breath. A crystal ball. Large enough to be costly, rare enough to be puzzling. She hadn't ordered anything like it.

Skye carefully removed the sides of the Styrofoam shell and lifted it free. The bottom had been flattened so it wouldn't roll. Tilting it, she admired the way rainbows bloomed inside the flawless sphere, threads of gold and violet spiraling like frozen auroras. At the very top, a halo of light seemed to pulse faintly, as though it were aware.

She rotated it further. Ridges appeared beneath her fingers. A jawline. Eye sockets.

Her breath left in a sharp hiss.

A crystal skull.

Skye froze and pulled her hands away.

The shock punched through her—half fear, half awe. Crystal skulls belonged to tales of lost civilizations, not to her unpacking table three days before the longest night of the year.

For a heartbeat, the shop around her seemed to hush. No rustle of tissue paper from the front, no muffled ring of the register. Just her, the faint scent of rose incense, and the skull's serene, unblinking gaze.

Its eyes were not empty pits but polished hollows, catching the light like pools of still water. The faint carving of teeth curved into something like a knowing smile—neither mocking nor sinister, but impossibly patient.

Hello, Skye.

She jerked her head up. The voice was deep, warm, and entirely in her mind. Male.

I've been looking for you for a long time.

Skye's pulse stuttered. She half-laughed, half-snorted—a reflex against the prickling at her neck—and bolted through the curtain into the shop. The familiar sight of the apothecary shelves grounded her. Jars of herbs—mugwort, chamomile, rosehips—stood in tidy ranks. Candles in every shade of the season—cranberry red, forest green, deep midnight blue—rested beside crystals labeled in neat, looping script. Skye averted her eyes, not wanting to hear any more rocks talking to her at the moment.

Her breath came shallow. She'd handled haunted jewelry, cursed tools, even the occasional wayward spirit. But this...

From the front of the shop, Sorcha glanced back, brows drawn in question. Skye shook her head—nothing. Nothing she could explain out here, at least.

She squared her shoulders and pushed back through the curtain. She approached the table slowly as if she were dealing with a skittish horse. The skull sat silent now, exuding a circle of peace.

And tucked up beside it was Rose, Thistle's sister, purring madly.

"Stars above," Skye whispered.

Named for the gray rosettes in her coat, the tabby opened one amber eye to look at her, then closed it again, redoubling her rumbling purr.

Well, that was a good sign.

She bent to retrieve the box lid. The shipping label was smeared, the sender's name lost in a gray blur of rain-wicked ink. Holding it at different angles, she squinted at the smeared letters. She couldn't make out anything. The sticker for Star, Stone & Flower had the correct address, that much she could tell. Then she noticed the label was pasted over a previous one. Maybe this would solve the mystery. She worried at the edge with her fingernail, managing only to rip both layers at once.

A flashlight revealed little—perhaps an *A*... or the curve of a *w*—

but nothing more. Jade could take it to the police lab, but Skye knew better than to cross that line.

Skye hissed in frustration and Rose returned the favor.

"Sorry, sweetie."

The cat gave her a slow blink, then closed her eyes and resumed her—meditation? Was that what she was doing?

Leaving Rose with her new friend, Skye went back through the curtain and found the store teeming with people. She'd have to help out. Before she could move, Sorcha appeared beside her, breathless. "What's the matter?"

Skye hesitated. Cillian was at the register, but his glance kept flicking toward them between customers.

"Nothing," she said, keeping her voice low so the customer sniffing the candles nearby couldn't hear.

"I felt it," Sorcha insisted. "A huge burst of energy. Then you came through that curtain like a banshee."

Skye lowered her voice. "What kind of energy?"

Sorcha's eyes softened, her voice almost reverent. "Celestial."

The word landed like a pebble in a deep well, ripples spreading through Skye's thoughts.

"What is it?" Sorcha asked.

"You'd better come see."

Luna had joined Cillian at the counter, freeing Sorcha to follow. Skye swept the curtain aside and led her to the long packing table.

The young seer stopped short. "A crystal ball—no, it's a skull."

"He," Skye said before she could stop herself.

Sorcha blinked. "Why 'he'?"

"It spoke to me."

Sorcha edged closer, the rainbow light from the overhead spot breaking over her face. "You'd think a skull would be creepy," she murmured, "but he feels peaceful. Benevolent."

"Rose sure likes him."

Sorcha placed a hand on each side of the head, carefully sliding one between the cat and the crystal. Nobody ever could tell when Rose would take exception and give them a swat.

The cat let out a protesting sound, then settled against Sorcha's hand. Her palms open on the sides of the skull, she closed her eyes. Sorcha's expression softened further, her breathing deepening into a meditative rhythm.

After a minute, she opened her eyes. "He doesn't talk to me. But he sent me...something. Warmth. Calm."

Skye nodded slowly. "We'll have to research him. I don't know what culture he's from."

"We could ask Iona. Or Minh," Sorcha offered.

"Good ideas. I'll talk to Dana first. Ask her if Minh can check. Jade might have some ideas. But mostly, we need to find how the heck he got here in the first place."

"What do we do with him in the meantime?"

Skye looked down at the skull, its rainbow-lit features serene, the cat still purring beside it.

"I'll put him in the safe overnight," she said quietly. "I hope he doesn't mind the dark."

CHAPTER

TWO

That evening, Skye cradled a warm mug of hot chocolate between both palms, letting the rising steam curl against her face. The fire popped and hissed in the hearth, throwing out waves of heat and an occasional burst of sparks that danced briefly before vanishing into the stone chimney. Outside, the sleet had thickened, tapping a steady rhythm on the cottage windows, as though impatient to be let in. She tried to wrap her head around what had happened at the shop earlier, but the day's images swirled as restlessly as the storm.

Her thoughts drifted to Jade, who even now was driving through this mess. Raised under magnolia skies and summer thunderstorms, Jade still thought snow was something best admired on a postcard. Yet she had taken the advanced law enforcement driving course and passed with top honors, proud enough to brag that she could spin her cruiser around like in the movies. "So don't worry," she'd told Skye. Easy to say. Not so easy for Skye to believe while ice was slicking the roads.

She took a slow sip, letting the rich taste of cacao linger, earthy and bittersweet, and tried to swallow down her anxiety with it. The dogs—Taran and Ashe—had been joined by two more farm hounds tonight, all of them forming a loose circle around the fire as though they were ancient guardians of the hearth. The beagle's snore rose and fell like a soft saw cutting through wood. Gandalf, the old barn cat, licked each paw with fussy precision before curling into a compact circle, tucking his nose beneath his tail. Skye's heart softened—she was glad the venerable creature had chosen to live out his twilight years inside, away from the drafty barns and cold rain.

Another log cracked with a sharp report. Taran sprang up, barked once, then eyed the log suspiciously before resettling with a huff. The moment of levity eased Skye's tight shoulders a little further, though her mind kept circling back to the crystal skull. She saw plenty of skulls around Samhain, and the bright sugar skulls in the Mexican neighborhoods for the Day of the Dead, painted with flowers and joy. To most Americans, skulls screamed horror, Halloween, and death. To the Mexicans, they were remembrance, love made visible. She wondered where Jade's family would place them on that spectrum. She doubted they were part of Santería practice—but still, the question tugged at her.

Headlights cut through the sleet, brushing across the curtains before swinging into the drive. Relief swept over her chest even before the car door slammed and heavy steps crunched on the porch. The front door swung wide, carrying a gust of damp air and Jade's familiar energy with it. The dogs surged forward in a happy mob, tails thumping against walls and legs, each one angling for their share of attention.

The knot of worry inside Skye loosened. She lifted her mug in greeting, her smile warmed by the firelight. "How were the roads?"

"Not bad," Jade said, scratching the dogs one by one. Her cheeks were flushed from the cold, her dark curls damp with melted sleet. "That course helped a lot."

"How was your shift?"

Jade tugged off her puff jacket and hung it on the peg by the door before kneeling at the gun safe. The metallic click of the lock punctuated the cozy sounds of the room. "Why can't people behave, at least for Christmas? A bunch of teenagers jumped an old lady. Ten dollars in her purse and a couple of presents—and they put her in the hospital for it."

"Is she all right?"

"Broke her wrist. Bruised all over." Jade unlaced her boots with a sigh, then looked up, the shadow in her eyes darker than the circles beneath them. "And the thefts—double what they were last year. Purse snatchings, bags ripped right out of hands, even in the malls."

"Think it's because people are losing benefits?" Skye asked quietly.

"Some." Jade stood, stretching until her back popped, then crossed the room and bent to kiss the crown of Skye's head. "But it's more than that. Entitlement. Some men who think the world should belong to them. Shoving people, picking fights over nothing." Her jaw tightened as she said it, the words bitten off.

"I've seen a few myself." Skye's shop had its share of would-be moral crusaders—strangers who came to glare too close, spit scripture, and threaten to "shut you down."

Jade's voice dropped low, ladened with anger and sadness. "People think they can say just about anything to me. Call me names. I'm getting sick of it."

It wasn't like Jade to admit the toll. Skye reached over, squeezing her arm with quiet certainty. "Oh, sweetie. I'm sorry. You'll get that detective promotion."

"Maybe." Jade raked a hand through her hair, the weariness of the day settling over her shoulders. "I'm going to shower. Wash it all off."

Skye called after her as she disappeared into the bedroom. "Potato leek soup on the stove. Fresh bread from the big house."

"Sounds perfect," came Jade's faint reply, softened by the hum of water starting in the pipes.

Skye ladled steaming soup into a deep bowl, the fragrant steam curling up to mingle with the wood smoke of the fire. She slid two slices of bread onto a small plate, still warm from the oven, and set out Aunt Nia's goat cheese spread—creamy and sharp, whipped with herbs grown right there on the farm. The tangy scent carried the memory of Yule feasts and long tables crowded with kin.

Jade emerged from the bedroom, damp curls clinging to her cheeks, her face flushed from the shower. She'd traded her uniform for soft flannel pajamas, the plaid rumpled and cozy, and—Skye had to bite her lip to keep from laughing outright—her tough, no-nonsense cop of a wife padded out in bunny slippers. Jade caught the look and raised an eyebrow, but her grin gave her away. "Ah, much better."

"Food, madam," Skye said with mock formality, sliding the bowl toward her.

Jade plopped into her chair and picked up her spoon, inhaling the soup like it was salvation.

"What do you want to drink?" Skye asked.

"How about some of that Frambozen?" Jade's eyes lit. The raspberry brown ale was one of their holiday traditions, as much a part of the season as fir boughs and twinkle lights.

Skye poured two mugs of the ruby-brown ale, the fruity tang rising as she set them on the table. For a few moments, the only sounds were the clink of spoons against bowls, the low crackle of fire, and the steady rhythm of sleet at the windows. Slowly, Jade's shoulders eased, the tension of her shift softening as the soup and bread worked their healing magic.

"Shop crowded?" she asked, pushing her empty bowl aside with a satisfied sigh.

"Jam-packed," Skye said, sipping her beer. "Good for the bottom line, if we can survive the madness."

A hush fell over the room, the kind of quiet only winter evenings seemed to carry—deep, layered, broken only by the fire's crackle and the beagle's soft snores from his cushion. Skye's lips curved. One of the children had christened him Flop, and she could still hear their giggles as the name stuck.

Jade watched her. "It's good to see you smile. But I can tell something's weighing on you."

Skye's smile faded, but she nodded. "Something really strange happened at the store today."

"Isn't that par for the course?"

"This one's top ten weird," Skye admitted. "Maybe even number one."

Jade leaned back, then rose and crossed to the sofa, patting the cushion beside her. Skye joined her, carrying their beers, and they nestled together. The small fir tree in the corner glowed with soft lights, its earthen pot waiting to be replanted on Twelfth Night in honor of the wise ones. The Yarrow clan always stitched their holidays together—threads of old pagan rites, Christian customs, and popular traditions woven into something uniquely theirs.

Ashe hopped up and muscled between them, her wolf blood showing in the sheer weight she flopped into Skye's lap. Skye let out a grunt. "If you insist," she muttered, shifting to make room.

Jade rubbed the dog's head until Ashe's eyes drooped, then stretched her arm along the back of the sofa. "So, give. What's the strangest thing that's ever happened at the shop?"

Skye drew out the story, savoring the telling—how the package had arrived, how ordinary it seemed, and then the hidden surprise at the bottom. She described turning the crystal, the shock of finding a face carved within. Jade's eyes widened, disbelief flickering into awe.

"A skull carved out of a crystal ball?"

"Exactly." Skye nodded, a little thrill running through her. The telling made it real in a new way. "But that's not the strangest part."

Jade sat cross-legged, Ashe grumbling but shifting to accommodate. "Do tell."

"It talked to me."

At first, Jade just nodded—then froze. "Sorry, what?"

"It told me it had been looking for me."

"Now that's creepy."

Skye laughed softly. "Startled me too. But...it didn't feel evil. It radiated peace. Wisdom, even." She told Jade how Rose had curled up beside it, unbothered, as though she'd found an old friend.

"Well, if Wild Rose approves." Jade's lips quirked into a smile.

Skye chuckled, but Jade's practical side surfaced quickly. "Did you call the shop that sent the incense?"

Skye slapped her forehead. "Earth and sky. I didn't even think of that."

"Guess the talking head distracted you."

"I'll do it first thing tomorrow."

"You kept the labels?"

"I did."

"Maybe I'll take them by the lab. See if Delila can figure out what's underneath." Jade stretched. "I'll find a time to drop by"

"And meet Mr. Crystal yourself?"

"Why not?" Jade teased. "Think he'll talk to me?"

"I hope so. Then I'll know I'm not losing my mind."

"You're not," Jade said simply, giving her hand a squeeze.

Warmth flooded Skye, though her next yawn nearly cracked her jaw. Jade stood and clapped her hands softly. "All right, dogs. Outside."

None of the pack moved. With a groan, Skye rose and shuffled to the door, the dogs finally rousing to follow her out. The cold air wrapped around them, sharp and damp, as sleet whispered against the porch roof and pattered softly onto the frozen ground. She tucked her arm through Jade's, leaning against her as they stood together.

Above, the gibbous moon sailed between tattered clouds, silvering the garden paths and turning the meadow into a pale expanse of white, the sleet layering it in a shimmering crust. The world held its breath, suspended in luminous stillness. Skye pressed closer to Jade, treasuring the peace of that moment, even as some instinct whispered that such calm could not last.

CHAPTER

THREE

S kye arrived at Star, Stone & Flower early, slipping through the back door before the deluge of customers began. Three days until the winter solstice, with Christmas following right after —it was about to be a madhouse. But for now, the shop was quiet, cloaked in the soft hum of the building waking with her. She set down her tall mocha, the paper cup leaving a dark ring on the counter, and spun the dial of the safe. Metal clicked, the door swung wide, and a familiar, uncanny face looked back at her.

Skye pulled out Mr. Crystal with both hands, his weight cool and solid, and set him carefully on the table. She flicked on the overhead light. The beam struck the skull's dome, scattering prisms across the wall. For the briefest moment, she could have sworn the sockets narrowed against the sudden brightness, as though the skull squinted. A trick of the light...or something more?

She leaned in, letting her gaze follow the rainbow fractures spider webbing beneath the surface. Just behind the right socket bloomed a starburst crack, with two more fissures tracing like fault lines toward the back of the skull. Whoever had carved him had possessed almost otherworldly patience—one wrong strike and the whole sphere would have shattered.

Turning him slowly, she watched streams of color shift with the light—ribbons of lavender and azure, sparks of gold, pools of amber as deep as honey. Its crown was capped in milky white, smooth and rounded like a yarmulke. Skye's lips curved. "Should I call you Rabbi?" she teased.

A faint spark leapt within the quartz, flickering like a firefly. Skye jerked back. Was that an answer?

Shaking off a shiver, she bent to check the delivery box again. This time, she found a packing slip caught beneath a fold of cardboard. She tugged it free and found the familiar Summit New Age Supply logo at the top. Everything listed—incense, holders, and the cheerful Christmas suncatchers—matched their order. Everything but the crystal skull.

Summit was based on the East Coast, which meant someone was already at a desk. Skye grabbed the store's cell and dialed, sipping mocha while the line rang. Someone answered and Skye introduced herself, mentioning her store name, then asked to speak with whoever had packed her box. She gave them the order number. After three rounds of a tinny Christmas song about Santa coming down the chimney tonight, someone picked up.

"This is Janice. Did you have an issue with your order?"

"Janice, this is Skye from Seattle."

"Hey, girl. How you holdin' up?"

"Crazed, but that's normal this time of year. And you?"

"Our rush was over weeks ago. It's been smooth sailing since early November. You're lucky you caught me—we're about to close until next year."

"I just wanted to double check our order," Skye said lightly.

"Is there a problem?"

"Not exactly. Did you happen to send a crystal item by mistake?" Her throat tightened around the words. She couldn't quite bring herself to say 'human-sized crystal skull.'

"Crystal? Like small, tumbled stones?"

"Bigger. A ball."

"Huh, I'd remember that." Skye heard typing on the other end, quick clicks against a keyboard. "Let's see. That order shipped in early November. You just got it yesterday?"

"Yep. Big delay."

"Not surprised. That's the fourth one like it this month. Tariffs, shortages—it's chaos. I'm sorry. Hope it doesn't hurt you."

"Oh, the incense will burn right off the shelves," Skye reassured.

"Ha, ha." Janice said, her voice deadpan.

"But no crystal ball?" Skye pressed.

"Not on my screen. And trust me—I've got a soft spot for quartz. I would've noticed." A pause. "If you don't want it, you can send it back, but I can't guarantee a refund."

"We'll keep it for now."

"All right. If anyone calls wondering about a missing crystal ball, I'll let you know."

"Appreciate it. Have a wonderful holiday, Janice."

"Same to you." Janice ended the call.

The backdoor opened. Skye glanced back and saw Sorcha, her steps light as if approaching an altar. "You beat me to him."

Skye chuckled. "Wanted a little session before the chaos begins?"

"He gives me a lift," Sorcha admitted, gazing at the skull with reverence. "Peace before the storm."

"It'll be busy, no doubt." Skye pushed back her chair. "I called Summit New Age Supply."

"And?"

"Everything else came from them, but not Rabbi Crystal here."

Sorcha blinked. "Rabbi?"

"Look at his crown. Like he's wearing a little cap."

Leaning in, Sorcha studied the milky dome, her lips curving. "We should ask him his real name."

"Don't you go naming a stray skull," Skye warned. "You'll get attached."

"Like Thistle and Rose?"

"Touché," Skye admitted with a laugh.

"Jade's coming later to take the label to the lab," she added. "See if anything's hidden underneath. For now, I think he stays."

Sorcha reached out, not quite touching the crystal, as though the air around him was sacred space. Her eyes softened. "Good. He feels...like he belongs here. I think I'm already attached."

A warmth seemed to settle around them, subtle but unmistakable, like the hush of snow falling outside or the stillness before dawn. Skye felt her chest ease, her earlier unease giving way to a quiet certainty. Whatever Mr. Crystal was, he wasn't here to harm. He was here to guide.

Skye opened an hour early during the winter holiday season and customers were already waiting for her to unlock the door.

"Welcome, welcome. Come out of the cold. Let us know if you need any help."

People scattered though the store, the pending deadline for gift buying nipping at their heels. Skye returned to the cash register, letting Sorcha reshelve books and straighten tables after rushed customers left chaos behind where order had reigned. It was a continual battle this time of year.

More people arrived and just before things got unmanageable, Luna pushed back the curtain from the back of the store followed by Cillian carrying two cappuccinos, if Skye remembered their favorite. "Traffic," Luna murmured when she got close to the front. "Sorry."

Skye pointed to the drinks. "Forgiven if you brought us some."

"Left two in the back."

Just as she said this, Sorcha pushed through the swirly curtain carrying two more tall cups. She handed Skye one. "Here's your mocha, no cream."

"But it's almost Solstice. I think whipped cream is called for."

Luna chuckled. "I'll amend your order for next time."

Skye leaned over and caught a whiff of mint from Sorcha's coffee, then took a sip of the still hot mocha. She'd been up early and the caffeine was welcome. The next couple of hours flew by with questions from customers, restocking and straightening products, and ringing up sales. Both registers were busy and this made Skye's heart sing. Maybe she and Jade could take a trip in February to somewhere sunny. Get out of the rain.

Brenna ran in from Old World Apothecary just down the street asking to change a stack of twenties. "People are using more cash this year," she said.

Sorcha nodded sagely, as if she'd been at this for years rather than a few months. "There's a movement to stop giving money to the banking billionaires. It's good for us. Fewer surcharges."

Cillian stepped up. "I'll run to the bank for more change. Anything else?"

Skye popped her head around one of the bookshelves. "A mocha. This one with whipped cream."

Cillian laughed. "Got it."

Skye returned to straightening out the spirituality section, enjoying the relative quiet in this corner. Then something changed. She felt the shift in energy before the bell above the door of the shop rang with an uncharacteristically discordant note. Skye stepped from behind the bookshelf.

In walked a tall, thin man dressed in an immaculately tailored three-piece suit of charcoal gray wool. His waistcoat gleamed with a subtle brocade, and a silver watch chain looped neatly across it. A starched collar framed a silk cravat of deep sapphire, fastened with a pearl pin. Polished leather shoes whispered across the floorboards, and he leaned lightly on an ebony cane capped with silver. A bowler hat, brushed to perfection, rested in one gloved hand.

The man paused just inside the threshold, his presence commanding yet understated, as though he had stepped out of another century and into her shop. His dark eyes swept the store with a measured elegance, and the chatter of customers faltered for the briefest moment.

His eyes came to rest on Skye. When he spoke, his voice carried the crisp, cultured tones of old England. "Good morning," he said with a small inclination of his head.

"Please feel free to look around," she said as if he were an ordinary customer. He most decidedly was not.

"I believe I am in the right place," she heard him mutter to himself.

What the heck did that mean? But Skye maintained her professional demeanor. "Let us know if you need anything."

The gentleman—how else could she describe him—gave her gracious nod and began a circumambulation of the shop, tilting his head from time to time as if sussing out a scent in the air or a frequency carried on the ethers.

She started to fold her hands but realized she was still holding a book in one. Skye stuffed the book onto a random shelf—she'd find its rightful home later—and made her way to the register where Sorcha and Cillian were staring at him between customers. Luna had taken up a more discreet surveillance next to the row of herbs in the apothecary section. The air was alive with psychic energy, so charged it would ignite if someone lit a flame.

"Stop staring," Skye whispered to the teens. "We don't want him to know we're watching him."

"We've got cameras," Cillian said to Sorcha in an undertone.

She nodded, then snapped to attention when a customer cleared her throat. Sorcha took the woman's items and asked at a normal volume, "Did you find everything you were looking for?

"I always find exactly the right thing for my sister and a few friends. This is such a great store," the woman emoted, somehow resetting the energy of the store back to normal.

But Skye kept watch and she could see Luna had her eye on him as well. The man kept circling back to the crystal and gemstone table, passing his hand over the trays of each kind, nodding to himself. A customer caught Skye before she could walk back toward the gemstones, asking to see the necklaces in the jewelry counters. He kept asking to see another, then another one, asking detailed questions about the qualities of the stones, the metal used in the setting, even who the craftsperson had been. She had to keep careful track of the jewelry, not leaving too many pieces out of the cases. Some were quite valuable—not like the Hope diamond or anything, but with some high-quality gems.

In the middle of this demanding sale, Skye looked up and realized the man had disappeared. She must have missed him leaving. Her shoulders fell a few notches in relief. There'd been something about him. But then she saw him emerge from the swirly curtain that separated the store from the private reading area and her shoulders climbed to her ears. What was he doing back there?

Luna followed right on his heels, saying something to him. Skye couldn't hear but assumed she was explaining the area was private. Maybe asking him if he'd like to book a reading. For some reason, Skye knew he was skilled enough to read for himself. He didn't need any help in that department.

Her customer put both his broad hands on the glass counter, recapturing her attention. "I can't decide between these two—the ruby and the amethyst."

Blast, after all this back and forth, she might lose the sale. "Those two stone have very different qualities. Let me know if you need more information."

He nodded. "I'm going to think about it. Check out her fancy dresses to see what color she might prefer." He gave her a wink.

"Certainly," Skye said, keeping upbeat. After all, the two registers behind her had been humming along all day, and it wasn't all about money to her. She'd been able to do quite a bit of teaching today in little exchanges. Explain how to ground and center before doing a reading. What different scents of incense were best for clearing a room and enhancing dreams. Found several books about the history of indigenous European traditions, on spell work, two on pagan Yule traditions. This was her true joy.

The English gentleman, as she'd dubbed him, left the store. He paused and put up his voluminous umbrella before stepping into the drizzle. The customer she'd been helping left right after him. Skye watched them outside. They headed off in the same direction but walked separately, not exchanging any words or a glance. A sudden suspicion came over her. What if the man shopping so intently for a necklace had been meant to distract her from the other one? Why had he gone into the back room? She'd have to ask Luna if she'd gone with him or discovered him wandering alone back there? What had he been after and what had he meant by his remark when he first came into the store—that said he thought he was in the right place?

Another customer pushed through the door and this time the bell rang true and clear. The sound of hectic, but happy shoppers grew louder, as if their voices had been muted before. The jubilant, boisterous holiday spirit had returned. Skye's shoulders resumed their normal position and her breath came more easily. She walked back toward Luna to ask what had happened, but a customer grabbed her on the way with a question about some of the goddess figurines. Then someone wanted advice on a book explaining magic to children. A kid wanted a magic wand. Once Skye helped him chose, he started waving it around shouting phrases from Harry Potter.

"Let me have that before you knock something over, George," his mother said, taking it with some difficulty from the child's hand.

Skye gave her a sympathetic smile. She'd have to catch up with Luna back at the farm.

CHAPTER

FOUR

"I mean, he was seriously strange. Like he stepped out of the last century," Skye said, stirring cream into her coffee as if that could dilute the memory.

"The twentieth?" Dana asked with a grin, spearing three hash-browns on her fork like a woman on a mission. She dunked them shamelessly into a pool of ketchup.

"Oh, that's right. I mean the nineteenth. Victorian, right Laurie?"

Laurie smiled sleepily from the comfort of her forest-green puff vest, looking as if she'd been poured straight from bed into the corner booth. She nodded, then took another long sip of her coffee. Rosa, curled up under the table, snored softly against her boot.

They'd met for an early breakfast at Dana's favorite Fremont cafe, a cozy spot strung with twinkling white lights and paper snowflakes that dangled from the ceiling fans. The air smelled of sizzling bacon and fresh cinnamon rolls, and a scraggly Christmas tree in the corner leaned under the weight of too many mismatched ornaments. Outside, a misty drizzle blurred the windows, the kind of gray Seattle morning that made coffee taste even better.

Too early, in Skye's opinion, but holiday shop hours demanded sacrifices, and Dana's schedule left dinner a lost cause. Lunch was no better—a sandwich half-eaten between phone calls, or more often, skipped altogether. Or something she forgot altogether.

Skye studied Laurie with mock suspicion. "You're half asleep. What were you up to last night?"

Laurie only burrowed deeper into her vest, her smile spreading.

"That good, huh?" Dana poked her under the table, one eyebrow raised.

Laurie shifted in her chair. "Wouldn't you like to know."

"I've sworn off men for the foreseeable future," Dana declared primly. Her recent divorce still clung to her like a stubborn perfume. "Drink your coffee."

For a minute, the only sound was the clink of silverware and the comforting hiss of the espresso machine behind the counter, followed by Bing Crosby crooning carols from the speakers. Skye finally broke the silence, hoping to glean some info from her brainy friends. "So...have either of you ever heard of crystal skulls?" She pitched her voice in the way one might announce they'd adopted a pet dragon.

Laurie perked up a bit, sitting forward to tackle her spinach and feta omelet. "Not me."

Skye eyed the golden square of eggs and cheese enviously. Her own plate of Greek scramble was tasty enough, but still—food envy was real.

Dana swallowed another mouthful. "I think the Tibetan monks use them. Don't know what for."

"And you think this odd customer has something to do with the crystal you got by mistake?"

Skye almost admitted that the skull didn't consider it a mistake at all, then thought better of it. Her friends accepted her empathic streak and her witchy family quirks, but she wasn't eager to sound like she'd completely gone round the bend. "Maybe. I mean, it felt like he threw a wet blanket over the shop's energy. Even the doorbell rang off-key."

"Maybe he just has bad vibes," Dana suggested, unconcerned.

"Then the case is terminal. He gave me the heebie-jeebies."

Laurie spread huckleberry jam thick across her toast, the purple goo glistening dangerously at the edge. Rosa's eyes lit up, though Skye suspected the dog had omelet ambitions. "So, this thing was just at the bottom of a box? And the company swears they never sent it?"

"Said they had no record of it. But we kind of like him."

"Him?" they both asked in unison.

"Yeah, feels like a 'he.' Wild Rose loves him."

"Well, if the cat approves..." Laurie's toast hovered midair, jam sliding ever closer to her fingers.

"Up for any research?" Skye asked, bright-eyed.

Dana chewed furiously before answering. "Senator Whitmore's up to her ears rolling out Americare for All. I'm drowning in briefs. I could ask Maxwell to poke around."

"That would be great," Skye said.

Laurie dabbed her mouth, her professor's composure returning. "John is presenting information on the increase of the salmon run with the renewal of the dams on the Klamath River to the FERC."

Skye's forehead wrinkled. "FERC?"

"Oh, Federal Energy Regulatory Commission."

"Why is this such a big deal?" Skye asked. "I mean everybody likes salmon, but—"

Laurie launched in, fork gesturing like a wand. "Southern Resident orcas are endangered. The dams block salmon runs, their primary food. With fewer salmon, the orcas are starving. Add in pollution, boat traffic, gutted environmental laws..." Her fork waved dramatically, a piece of egg flinging to the floor, where Rosa claimed it triumphantly.

Before Laurie could build up steam, Skye cut in with a sly smile. "So, your research is really important."

Laurie laughed, catching herself. "Okay, I'll spare you."

"I really need some advice about this crystal skull," Skye said.

Laurie cocked her head, thinking. "Have you asked that woman with the antique shop?"

"Who?" Dana asked.

"You know, the one who owns Artifacts & Antiquities."

"Right, the place with the Romanov ghost you helped over," Skye said.

"I remember that. Naomi—is that her name?" Dana said.

"Niamh Butler." Some people remembered faces, but Skye had always had a knack for remembering names.

"She might know something." Dana shoveled in more potatoes. Skye marveled—as always—that Dana could eat like a linebacker and still stay skinny, while Skye's body had settled into what she called "pillow chic." She was well past worrying about societal rules for female bodies. The farm and shop kept her strong.

"Good idea," Skye said. "I'll give her a call, if she isn't buried in holiday madness." She checked her phone and sighed. "Speaking of madness, I need to get to the shop before the hordes descend."

She dropped some cash on the table, scratched Rosa's head, and with a last wave, headed into the chilly Seattle morning. The sidewalks glistened with rain, shoppers bustled past in puffy coats with red-and-green shopping bags, and the coffee cart across the street was already hawking hot cider. Skye tugged her scarf tighter, ready to face the festive chaos waiting at Star, Stone & Flower.

TRUE TO HER WORD, a few customers had already lined up outside the store when Skye drove by. The fog still clung to the edges of the U District, softening the outlines of streetlamps and parked cars, giving the morning an otherworldly hush. She parked in her spot in the back, the air sharp with cedar and damp leaves, and let herself in through the rear door.

The first thing she did—before lights, before registers, before unlocking the front—was take out the crystal skull from the safe. As she lifted him free, refracted rainbows shimmered across the walls. He beamed at her, not with eyes but with an unmistakable presence.

"Good morning, Skye Fiosa Yarrow."

Skye laughed at the formality, her full name rolling through the quiet shop like a blessing. "And what should I call you?"

"My name is Anuun."

She lingered over the sound, tasting its resonance. "What a beautiful name. Does it have a meaning?"

"The closest in your language is *Father Sun*."

"Stars above," Skye whispered.

"Want to prepare for the day with a quiet moment?"

"That's a good idea. It will be a busy one."

"If you'd like, put your forehead against mine and we can hum together."

Skye hesitated. She should probably cleanse the artifact first. But "artifact" felt wrong—Anuun radiated awareness, kindness, a steady golden peace. Consciousness itself seemed to gather around him, humming in the still air. She drew a breath, then leaned forward until her brow rested against cool crystal.

At once, a low tone vibrated through her bones, a sound deeper than words. She joined him, humming, their voices blending—hers soft and human, his resonant as if it came from the very heart of the stone. The vibration smoothed the static of her morning rush and lulled her into stillness. The world fell away until there was only breath, sound, and a widening silence.

A delicate chime, like glass struck by sunlight, brought her gently back. She felt rested, centered, her spirit polished as if by invisible hands. "Thank you, Anuun."

"My pleasure, Deep Knower."

Heat rose to her cheeks. She didn't feel like she deserved the title, but some part of her thrilled to it. Rising to her feet, Skye left the safe's glow and walked toward the front of the store, the bell over the door already trembling with the promise of the day.

She rose still wrapped in the glow of silence, her pulse slow and steady, the air around her humming faintly as if the crystal's resonance lingered in the walls. Skye carried that serenity with her, each step like moving between worlds.

The moment she unlocked the door, the enchantment broke with the creak of hinges and a rush of cold, damp Seattle air. The bell jangled overhead, loud and ordinary, and life came tumbling in. Within minutes, chaos reigned.

Seattleites bustled through the doorway in fleece and puffy jackets, coffee cups clutched like holy relics. One woman sighed as her phone buzzed, another muttered about parking, and someone's toddler dropped a goldfish cracker that instantly crumbled into orange dust on the mat.

Skye's lips twitched. From crystalline hums and titles like *Deep Knower* to spilled snacks and wet boots—all before nine a.m., and one—Skye noted with a blink—looked like she'd come straight from a Halloween ball.

The woman swanned in as though she owned the place, the bell over the door jangling indignantly at her grand entrance. She wore a floor-length gown of black velvet that seemed to drink in the light, its trailing sleeves whispering against the floorboards as she moved. A lace-up bodice pulled her bust into dramatic lines, and a hood framed her pale, powdered face like something conjured out of a gothic romance. A necklace of oversized glass beads clinked in theatrical punctuation against her corset, and every flick of her hand flashed chunky silver rings shaped like snakes, pentagrams, and crescent moons. Her eyelids glimmered with lavender shadow dusted in glitter, her lips a slick, unyielding midnight black. Even her boots—peeking out beneath the velvet hem—were dagger-toed and wickedly high-heeled.

A broomstick-shaped umbrella leaned against her shoulder, absurd and yet threatening, as if she'd ridden it in with the morning mist. But unlike Mary Poppins, there was no cheer in her step. A dark cloud that matched her costume seemed to hover about her, prickling against the warmth of the shop's twinkling lights and fragrant incense.

A guy in a fleece vest leaned toward his companion and whispered, "Did I miss the memo about costumes?"

Skye bit back a smile. "Solstice is coming soon. She seems to have dressed for the wrong occasion."

The rest of the customers, true to Seattle form, went about their business, pointedly pretending not to notice. The air smelled of beeswax candles and sandalwood, soft Celtic harp music weaving through the background, yet the velvet woman's presence soured it all, like smoke seeping under a door. She wafted around the store with exaggerated grace, lifting items as if testing their weight against some private measure, her head cocking at odd, almost animal angles. Skye thought of the hounds back on her family farm, sniffing the air when they caught a strange scent. The other customers gave her a wide berth, drifting unconsciously away from her path.

The registers soon demanded Skye's attention. Shoppers crowded forward, arms full of last-minute Solstice gifts—books of spells and crystals clinking together in baskets, bundles of sage and cedar tied with ribbon. Sorcha arrived to help, her calm efficiency soothing the press of bodies, and Skye waved Cillian to the second register. That freed her to fetch display items, answer questions, and keep the tide moving.

She was crouched behind the jewelry case, rearranging a tray of moonstone pendants, when a harsh, deliberate clearing of the throat grated through the cheerful hum. Skye looked up—and there she was.

The harridan loomed directly before her.

"Are you the proprietress of this establishment?"

The woman's voice was an ordinary American timbre, yet the vocabulary rang of Victorian England. Skye blinked. What was with the sudden influx of people who talked or dressed as if they'd stepped out of Dickens? Had some society club picked her store as

28

their meeting ground?

"Yes, ma'am." The words slipped out before Skye could stop them. This woman was no older than she was, but *ma'am* felt inevitable. "How may I help you?"

Amusement flickered over the woman's sharp features, replaced quickly by an expression of cultivated superiority. Her nose—long and aquiline—seemed perfectly designed for looking down at people. Skye bit her lip to keep from laughing.

"I wonder if you have any larger crystals," she said, folding her hands. Skye now saw that the hands were encased in black leather gloves too tight to be ornamental. The fingers curved in a way that suggested claws rather than nails.

"Or crystal figurines. Perhaps even a bust." Her words clattered with menace, a flock of dark birds gathering in the rafters.

Skye straightened, unease rippling through her.

"I ordered one from a dealer back east, but it hasn't arrived. An unconscionable delay considering the press of the holiday rapidly approaching." Her eyes narrowed, predatory, as she studied Skye.

Skye forced her features into neutrality, though she noticed the two teenagers at the registers staring, wide-eyed, their shock poorly concealed. She shot them a warning look.

The woman's spine snapped rigid, an eerie marionette jerk that made Skye half-expect to hear bones crack. Her pulse quickened. How could she possibly surrender Anuun—the sweet being who radiated blessing—to this creature cloaked in shadows?

"I'm sorry to hear that," Skye said smoothly. "You might try a crystal store. They'll have a wider selection."

The woman muttered something low, sharp, and unintelligible under her breath. Was it some kind of spell?

"If you'd like to leave your name and an email or phone number," Skye offered, "I could certainly let you know if something like that turns up." She prayed the line would hurry this one out before the kids betrayed her again.

The woman only stared. For a wild moment Skye braced herself for *I'll be back* in a Schwarzenegger snarl. The image nearly made her laugh, but the humor caught in her throat.

The woman leaned in close, her perfume a bitter mix of tuberose and cold stone. "I don't give my name to just anybody, witch."

Before Skye could respond, a sharp hiss cut through the air. Thistle, her sleek shop cat, appeared on the counter as if summoned by the tension. His fur stood on end, back arched in a perfect Halloween silhouette, tail lashing like a whip. His green eyes glowed, fixed unblinkingly on the velvet intruder.

The woman's lip curled, but she didn't flinch. With a swirl of black velvet, she turned and strode out, the bell clanging after her like a protest. The air seemed to lighten the moment she crossed the threshold, though a faint ripple of unease lingered in her wake.

Skye let out her breath. Thistle leapt down, twining around her ankles as if to reassure her: *I've got your back.* She thought Laurie would agree that's what the cat was saying.

CHAPTER

FIVE

L aurie made it to Artifacts & Antiques only five minutes late. John's meeting had run late and she couldn't skip out on him. Traffic was an impossible snarl. Once she reached Belltown, she ducked into a Northbean to use the facilities and bought an eggnog latte out of guilt. But why should she feel guilty? Northbean had millions of stores and made more money than maybe even Baldwin Cress. Close enough. She even grabbed a doggie biscuit for Rosa. Two to be precise.

Niamh was just ushering the last customer out and flipped her sign to *Closed* as Laurie scooted in. The little brass bell above the door gave a tired jingle, as if it had been through a hundred years of greetings. Shelves and glass cases glittered with curiosities—bronze astrolabes, jade figurines, tarnished silver goblets—like a half-forgotten museum where every object whispered of another century. The faint aroma of sandalwood incense hung in the air, mingling with the sharper tang of wood polished with lemon oil.

Niamh locked the door and said, "Your friend Skye is in the back office. Shall we?" She eyed Laurie's Northbean cup, and Laurie felt another stab of guilt. Why hadn't she bought more for her friends? Where was all this guilt coming from?

"Sorry, I should have brought two more. Traffic got me all flustered."

Niamh waved her hand and said in her Indian British accent, "Not to worry. I have chai in the back."

Laurie immediately regretted her latte. This woman might make killer chai. She followed her through a narrow passage that smelled faintly of cedar polish and candle wax. Past a curtained doorway, the shop gave way to a cozy office. A broad oak desk stood at the center, crowded with ledgers, teacups, and a brass lamp casting a warm glow. Walls were lined with bookshelves sagging under the weight of history—leather-bound volumes, brittle maps, and boxes stamped with the dust of faraway places.

On the desk, Natasha, the smoke gray Maine Coon, ruled her kingdom with icy disdain. She stared daggers at Rosa, who had trotted in hopefully, tail wagging. The little Havanese tried all her charms—head tilts, soft whines, a crouch-and-play bow—but Natasha remained unmoved, lifting her chin like a queen affronted by a jester. When Rosa finally stretched up to sniff her nose, the cat raised one elegant black paw in warning.

Niamh tutted. "Tash, behave. We are polite to our guests."

But Natasha only bared her teeth in a silent hiss, gleaming fangs sharp in the lamplight. Rosa promptly retreated to cower under Laurie's chair. Laurie reached down to stroke her ears, her heart tugged by the dog's disappointment. The poor girl only wanted to share her joy with everyone.

Niamh handed Skye a cup of chai, the steam curling fragrantly of cardamom and cloves, and asked Laurie if she wanted one. Laurie simply raised her paper cup in answer, and they all settled in.

Skye caught the antiquity dealer up on how the crystal had arrived and the strange visitors in her store who seemed to be looking for it.

"Another one?" Laurie said, tugging her chair a little closer to

Rosa, who still lingered beneath it like a child hiding behind her mother's skirts.

"She was there first thing when I got to the shop after breakfast." Skye described the woman, her hands sketching dark velvet and jangling beads in the air. "Wondered if we carried large crystal items, like a ball or—get this—a bust."

"Like a carved head?" Laurie asked, her eyes widening. Something about the phrase made her pulse quicken, though she couldn't have said why.

"Said an order she'd placed in early November never showed up. Practically threatened me, but Thistle ran her off."

"Thistle?" Niamh arched one perfectly penciled brow.

"One of the feral kittens we found. Jumped onto the counter and hissed at her."

I like that cat, Rosa sent up loyally. Laurie bent to brush a finger across her soft head.

"So, there's a stir in the metaphysical community."

"It would seem so. I really appreciate your help figuring this out, Niamh."

"I'm not sure how much help I'll be. A crystal skull, you say? I'm not an expert on Central American artifacts."

Skye leaned forward, excitement glimmering in her eyes. "Central American? See? You've already helped. I wasn't sure they came from that region."

Niamh rested her fingertips on the edge of her desk, rings flashing in the lamplight. "I believe so. The Tibetans use them as well. Is the crystal embedded with other gems?"

"No. Just clear quartz."

"Then it's not from the Tibetan tradition. More likely a Mayan artifact."

Skye tilted her head. "Thing is though, Cillian and Sorcha did some quick internet research when he arrived—"

"He?" Niamh cut in, but Skye waved her off.

"I'll get to that. When they searched, that AI that pops up these days and Wikipedia both claimed all the crystal skulls are modern. At least from the mid-nineteenth century. That many were carved in Germany when there was a lot of interest in ancient cultures."

She took another sip of chai, the warmth grounding her. "This is really good."

"My grandmother's recipe," Niamh said, her eyes softening for just a moment.

"They mentioned some town..." Skye searched her memory.

"Idar-Oberstein?"

"That's the one. Said a French antiquities dealer opened a shop and peddled them to gullible buyers. An ethnographer donated three to a museum in Mexico."

Niamh sighed, and the sound was like the settling of old wood in her office.

"The articles claim no crystal skulls have ever been found from documented excavations. That the New Age—" she drew mocking air quotes "—made up the whole story lock, stock and barrel."

"Documented." Niamh emphasized the word as if it carried weight Laurie hadn't noticed.

Skye studied her for a long moment. "I have to tell you, this skull doesn't feel like some knock-off from a crystal workshop."

A knowing smile curved Niamh's lips. "You refer to this crystal head as *he*. Want to tell me about that?"

Skye hesitated, glancing at Laurie. The office felt suddenly closer, the tick of a brass clock on the bookshelf loud in the quiet.

Laurie silently asked Rosa if they could trust this woman.

I like her, but not the cat, Rosa said.

Like is different from trust.

She wants to help, but she's hiding something. Nothing bad.

Niamh was still watching Skye, so Laurie made a so-so gesture with her hand.

Skye gave a tiny nod. "I can hear the skull in my mind, and the voice is male."

"Is this usual for you?"

"Not really. I'm an empath. Sometimes I hear a person's thoughts, but this is quite distinct. Very clear."

"What does this skull say about why he's arrived? About the people who've come looking for him?"

Skye blinked. A jolt of realization tightened her chest. She hadn't asked Anuun about that. She would as soon as she got back to the shop.

"If you don't want to say, that's understandable," Niamh said gently, though her eyes shone with curiosity.

"No, that's all right. He says he's glad to be where he is. He seems to feel like he belongs with us for now." Skye didn't share the rest—that he'd been searching for her, or the secret of his name.

Niamh settled back in her creaky wooden chair, fingers curled around her teacup. She took a long, slow sip as though bracing herself for a story.

"What you found on the internet is only what ordinary society is prepared to believe. These skulls are well known in metaphysical circles. They have been used by the Maya and the western mystery schools for ages."

The lamplight flickered across her face, throwing her eyes into shadow.

"I know a man who was given a crystal skull in Toulouse during World War II with the instruction to take it to safety. The Nazis were scouring Europe—" she shifted in her chair, bracelets chiming faintly "—even other parts of the world, for occult relics. Toulouse was the international headquarters for a few metaphysical schools. The Nazis sent a team to raid the treasures of their sanctuaries. The seat of one organization passed to this country until the danger on the continent was over."

Boy, had they come to the right place, Laurie thought. She glanced down at Rosa, who—judging the feline menace past—had curled up in a circle under her chair, finally asleep. The sight softened Laurie's chest, her worry replaced by a ripple of protectiveness.

"I'm sure you're familiar with the Ahnenerbe's search for the Spear of Longinus." Niamh's voice was low, expectant.

"Uh, not really," Skye admitted.

"The Spear of Destiny is the weapon that pierced Christ's side as he hung on the cross. Therefore, it has traces of his blood and is considered sacred to many Christians. The story goes that the artifact confers invincibility. The Ahnenerbe was established by Himmler to send agents around the world to search for occult objects."

"I guess Hitler never got it, then," Laurie quipped, her tone wry to cover unease.

"That is debatable on two fronts. First, they took the spear from the Imperial Treasury at the Hofburg Palace in Vienna, Austria—if indeed it was the real artifact." She ticked off the points with a long finger against the wooden arm of her chair. "Second, there is a legend that Hitler did not die in his bunker but escaped to Argentina."

Laurie snorted, but Niamh's steady gaze didn't waver.

"It is not as outrageous as it sounds. Many Nazis fled to that country. This is a matter of record. Plus, there are German enclaves and a lot of SS memorabilia has been discovered there."

"No kidding?" Skye shuddered, the motion running up her spine like a chill draft.

"This man I mentioned earlier who was given a skull to keep safe during the war."

"Right," Skye said.

"He enjoys the appellate of Dean of Crystal Skulls. He's studied them all his life. Found several on undocumented—" she let the word drop like a stone into the silence "—excavations. Lucky for you, he lives in Seattle."

As Niamh's words settled into the warm hush of the office, the brass lamp flickered, though there was no draft. Skye felt it then—a faint hum in her chest, the way a struck crystal bowl resonates in the bones. Anuun. The name surfaced unbidden. The sensation was sharper this time, not just presence but unease, a low vibration that raised the hairs along her arms.

Rosa stirred in her sleep, gave a small whine that faded into silence. Natasha's silver eyes flicked toward the humans, unblinking, her tail twitching once as though she, too, had caught the ripple of something unseen.

Skye wrapped both hands around her teacup, letting the heat anchor her, but in her mind the echo remained—not just patient and watching, but edged with disquiet.

CHAPTER
SIX

S kye woke up early the next morning and even beat Jade out of the house. On the way to her old green Subaru, Skye smelled cinnamon and sugar wafting from the big farmhouse. They were at it already. Baking for the big celebration in two days. The longest night, Winter Solstice. Called *An Grianstad* by her Irish ancestors, named for the three days that the sun stands still at its lowest point on the horizon.

She found Grandmother Moira just pulling a baking sheet out of the oven. "Aye, ye always had a nose for me cookin'. You'll be eating this whole plate if I don't keep an eye on ye."

Skye laughed and snagged a steaming bun. Grandmother Brigid kneaded more dough at the long table and her mother cut up vegetables across from her. "I think two King salmon," Cormac said, his finger poised over his phone, ready to place the order. "Is that enough?"

"Better make it three," Fíona said.

"It be *Oidhche nan Seachd Suipearan*," Moira declared, then inclined her head toward Angus, who sat at the last empty space at the table eating a plate of eggs and sausage. "He'll be wantin' to feast, he will."

"Everyone will," Skye said.

Her Scottish ancestors mostly stuck with calling this time of year Midwinter or Yule, taken from the Norse *Jól*, but in Scots Gaelic, it was called the Night of the Seven Suppers, because you could sit to eat that many times before the sun rose again.

"We all want to feast at Yule, Grandma." Skye leaned into kiss her, but Moira ducked.

"Ye'll not be getting that glaze all over my face. Get on with ye, now."

"Bring that new crystal home," her mother called as Skye walked out the door. "We've heard so much about it."

Skye took her prize out to the car and headed to Seattle behind her father, juggling the rest of the cinnamon bun in one hand and the steering wheel in the other. She wanted to meditate with Anuun before the wild rush of shoppers today. She smiled at his name. He'd said it meant *Father Sun*. Perfect for the rebirth of the sun this time of year. The modern Druids call it *Alban Arthan*, the light of Arthur, because the days started to get longer after the darkest night.

She pulled up to the back of the store, parked her trusty Subaru, and walked to the door. As soon as she inserted the key, the door pushed open by itself. Skye's blood ran cold. Then she caught herself. Didn't her mother always say never borrow trouble? Maybe Sorcha had forgotten to lock the back. She pushed through and ran to the safe where she'd stashed Anuun before she left.

The door hung open.

The safe was empty.

Not wanting to believe the skull had been stolen, Skye searched the back storage and the private reading room, turning over boxes and piles of packing material before she realized she might be destroying evidence if the worse was true. She called for him in her mind, sending out probing thoughts, listening carefully for an answer, any vibration from him.

Nothing.

Skye sank to the floor and put her head in her hands. Tears leaked from her eyes. How had she gotten so attached to this little beam of light in such a short time?

She pushed Jade's number.

"Hey, babe. I'm running late. Stuck in traffic."

"He's gone."

"Who's gone?"

"Anuun. The crystal skull." Skye told her about the back door being unlocked, finding the safe empty and her search. "He's not here."

"Call and report it," Jade said. "I'll call my sarg and see if he'll let me come."

Skye disconnected and with shaky hands dialed 911 and reported the theft.

"Are you in immediate danger?" the dispatcher asked.

"I think they're gone."

"Are you certain? Is anyone still in your store?"

Skye walked into the retail area and looked around. "I'm alone."

"Lock the doors. We'll have someone there as soon as we can."

Skye thanked her. A tall man peered through the window, a little girl beside him eagerly pointing at the stuffed magical creatures in the window. She couldn't close on solstice. The other shop helpers would be here soon.

Skye's nerves jangled as she waited, the shop too quiet for comfort. The cinnamon warmth of her grandmother's buns lingered faintly on her tongue, but the sweetness had curdled into dread. Every crystal on the shelves caught the morning light as if nothing had changed, yet the absence in her safe left the whole place hollow.

The police arrived twenty minutes later, their uniforms crisp, their notepads already open. They asked the questions she expected —when she'd last seen the crystal skull, who had keys to the back, whether she'd noticed anyone unusual hanging around. Skye answered as steadily as she could, though her throat tightened every time she said 'the skull.'

One officer dusted the safe for prints while the other checked the back door's lock. "No sign of forced entry," he said, his tone neutral but edged with skepticism. "Could be someone who knew their way in."

Skye bristled, then forced herself to breathe. "I lock up every night. My staff is careful. This wasn't an accident."

They took her statement. After Skye explained her discovery of the theft, the officer asked, "What is the value of this crystal?" The woman's pen hovered over her notebook.

Skye wondered how to answer this. "We were in the process of getting it appraised. It could be quite old. Perhaps an artifact from the ancient Maya."

The officer's pencil-thin eyebrow went up. "Seriously? But you're not sure?"

"We need an expert to authenticate it." Skye didn't want to say Anuun had just arrived unordered and unexpected.

The woman made another note, then closed her pad with a snap. They walked her through the paperwork. Sorcha and Cillian arrived in the middle of this, but the officers did not allow Skye to flip the shop sign to Open.

"Could one of you go tell the customers outside we've had an emergency and will be opening late?" Skye asked.

Once Cillian came back from this chore, he reminded Skye of the security cameras. She slapped her forehead. "I can't believe I forgot."

Cillian accessed the tapes with one officer looking over his shoulder. At night, they were set for motion detection only. They watched the cats chasing each other for a while, then set it on fast forward. The cats walked through a couple more times. Then Rose pounced on something and hunched to eat.

"Eww," Sorcha said, her face screwed up.

Skye hated to think they had mice, but if they did, it looked like the cats would take care of that problem.

The feed picked up again at 4:32 am. A shadowy figure in a bulky coat with a hood walked in, stood still for a while, turning their head around, then walked straight to the safe. The person took out a stethoscope and applied it to the safe's chest, then started turning the dial. After a few minutes, the figure opened the door and took out Anuun, who seemed distressed to Skye. She didn't mention this to the police. They already thought she was a little nuts.

When the figure turned, the ghost of a face showed for a split second. "There." Cillian sat back with a look of satisfaction. They watched the person place the skull in what looked like a padded carrier, then leave.

The officer handed Cillian a card. "Can you forward this file to us?"

"Sure thing."

"We'll file the report," the fingerprint gatherer said, his tone practiced. "Keep your doors secure—"

Skye bit her lip to keep from telling him they always did.

"—and if anything else seems off, call us right away."

By the time they finally left, it was almost noon. Sunlight poured through the shop's front windows, catching dust motes that drifted like tiny ghosts in the air. Luna had already prepared the registers and the kids, as Skye kept thinking of them, welcomed customers with profuse apologies.

"We had a break in. Nothing serious." They repeated what Skye had instructed them to say.

One woman went straight to the jewelry case and pointed at an emerald pendant. "Oh, thank heaven they didn't take this. I've had my eye on it and I'm getting it for myself for Yule."

Sorcha wrapped it carefully and Skye wished her a happy solstice, then went to the back room. She was no good with customers today. She heard the back door open again. For a panicked second, she thought the police had returned. Instead, Jade swept in, her dark hair mussed from the December wind, her eyes sharp and searching until they landed on Skye.

"Hey," Jade said softly, already pulling her into a solid embrace. "I came as soon as I could."

Skye clung to her, relief spilling through her chest. "They took him," she whispered. "The safe was empty. I don't know how—"

Jade leaned back, her expression steady but fierce. "Then we find out how. Whoever did this knew what they were after." She brushed her thumb across Skye's cheek, grounding her. "This isn't just some shiny trinket. You told me how important he is?"

Skye nodded, swallowing the ache in her throat. "There's someone who might help. The Dean of Crystal Skulls. If anyone knows where to start, it's him."

Jade's jaw set with determination. "Then that's our next stop."

Skye drew a long breath. "First, I want to get Rosa over here. Maybe Ashe, too. See if they can scent the thief."

Jade nodded. "I'll go get her, then. See you in about an hour."

"Thanks, sweetie. Don't know what I'd do without you." She hugged her tight.

Sunlight still streamed in, bright and defiant, but beneath it all she felt the empty space where Anuun should have been.

When Laurie and Rosa arrived at Star, Stone & Flower, the place was packed with customers. The witchy shop glowed with its usual cozy charm—warm lamplight, shelves glittering with crystals, and the faint hum of enchantment. A garland of rosemary and silver ribbon twined along the counter, and tiny crystal snowflakes hung from the ceiling, catching the light like bits of frozen magic. A cinnamon-and-clove candle flickered near the register, filling the air with holiday warmth. But Skye's face did not match the cheer.

"I can't believe this. I'm so sorry," Laurie said.

Skye nodded for Sorcha to take over explaining tarot cards to the customer she was helping and greeting Laurie. She looked down at

Rosa. "The skull was locked in the back room safe. No sign of forced entry. Whoever did it knew what they were after."

"Do you have any ideas about who did this?"

"No, but maybe Rosa can get a fix on the crook."

My nose is enough, Rosa said.

Laurie did not repeat this snarky comment to Skye but unclipped the little dog's leash. "All right, Agent Rosa," Laurie whispered. "Do your magic."

The bell jingled again as Jade appeared in the doorway, holding a leash attached to Ashe—the half-wolf husky from the farm. His pale eyes gleamed like moonlight, and his thick silver coat shimmered under the crystal lights.

"Thought you could use a real tracker," Jade said with a grin.

Rosa gave an indignant bark, as if to say *Excuse me?*

"Team effort," Laurie told them. "No turf wars."

Rosa gave a quick woof, tail high, and began her methodical inspection. The little dog circled the counter, snuffling around the register and under the stool where Skye usually perched. Then moved into the store—nose twitching over displays of candles and stones, then sneezing dramatically at a basket of sage bundles.

"She's clearing the air," Laurie explained, deadpan.

Skye managed a tight smile. "Either that or she's critiquing my supplier."

Customers glanced down at the little Havanese as she wound her way among them, one bending down to pet her. But Rosa ignored the young man. He looked disappointed.

"She's working," Laurie explained, as though the dog were a federal agent and not a ten-pound fluff ball.

"Oh," he said, a look of confusion on his face.

The bell over the door tinkled and Brenna popped in from Old World Apothecary carrying coffees for everyone. Rosa sniffed her shoes, then rose on hind legs to investigate her coat pocket.

"Rosa, if I'd known you were here, I would have brought you a dog biscuit," Brenna said.

I like what I smell, Rosa said to Laurie.

Brenna set the coffee on a nearby table, pulled a tiny cookie shaped like a star out of her pocket, and offered it to the little dog. Ashe joined them, and they made quick work of the treats.

Rosa trotted off, crumbs in her beard, professional demeanor temporarily compromised. She returned to sniffing—first the shelves, then the floor. She suddenly veered toward the back room, nose twitching furiously. On her way she paused at the feet of a customer, a woman in flowing tie-dye with a head full of silver curls. Rosa sniffed one sandal delicately, then barked once.

"Oh my!" The woman jumped. "What's happening?"

"She's an investigator," Laurie said, her mouth twitching up. "Routine questioning."

The woman blinked, then laughed. "Well, tell her I'm innocent, but she's welcome to check my aura."

Another customer adjusted a wreath-shaped headband that flashed red and green lights and said, "Maybe she's sniffing for gingerbread."

Ashe padded behind her in dignified silence, nose working methodically. Where Rosa zigzagged and sneezed, Ashe traced neat, deliberate circles, pausing once to sniff a shelf of obsidian.

"See?" Jade whispered to Skye. "Professional."

"Maybe," Skye murmured, "but Rosa's got flair."

Satisfied, Rosa moved on. Skye followed her into the private reading room where boxes were stacked in uneven towers. Rosa nosed through the packing materials until she came to one corner and froze. Her tail went straight out, then began to wag in slow, deliberate circles. Rosa trotted toward the staff door, following a trail. They trailed behind her. The air here was cooler, still faintly metallic with the scent of safe steel and packing tape.

Rosa went straight to the far corner where the heavy safe stood open, its door hanging like a wound. She sniffed the metal rim, the floor, the discarded bubble wrap. Her tail stiffened.

Too many people have been messing around here, she complained.

Then she sneezed twice, backed up, and let out a sharp bark. *Found it.*

"She's got something," Laurie said.

Ashe joined her, nose pressed close to the metal seam. Her hackles rose and a low rumble vibrated in her chest.

"She smells it too," Jade said quietly. "Whoever took that skull didn't belong in this room."

Rosa barked sharply in agreement, circling the safe as if to mark it for evidence.

Rosa followed the invisible trail to the side wall, nose pressed to the baseboard, then around the room—past the broom closet, the office, and the door leading to the alley. She paused there, sniffed once more, then barked low and steady.

"She's saying the scent goes out that door," Laurie said softly.

Skye's stomach twisted. "So, whoever it was cracked the code on the door, just like we thought."

Rosa sat back on her haunches, clearly proud of her deduction.

"She's got the scent," Laurie told Skye. "She'll be able to confirm the thief when we find him."

"Is it a man?"

Rosa caught Skye's eye and barked. Ashe seemed to agree.

Skye's eyes shimmered with gratitude. "Thank you. You've found our best lead yet."

A soft thump sounded behind them. Thistle, Skye's silver-gray cat, landed gracefully atop a stack of boxes. One was wrapped in red paper printed with silver stars—Skye's half-finished attempt at decorating gifts for her little cousins. Thistle eyed the curling ribbon. *Mortals and their shiny toys,* she sniffed. *I've spent the week rescuing ornaments from the tree.*

Rosa whipped around, nose twitching.

So, the dogs have confirmed what any competent feline could have told you from the beginning, Thistle said, his voice curling around Laurie's mind like silk.

Laurie translated for Skye.

"Oh, don't start," Skye told the cat. "They're actually helping."

Thistle began grooming a paw with exaggerated calm. *Helping? By flinging their scent everywhere?*

Has he smelled his litter? Rosa asked. Ashe stayed out of it, wisely.

Laurie grinned. "Rosa says she found the scent of someone who smelled like cheap cologne and dark magic. Probably a man."

Thistle stopped mid-lick. *Cologne, yes. The kind mortals wear to hide fear. And that magic...* He hopped down gracefully and padded toward the safe, nose twitching. A faint ripple of energy shimmered in the air around his whiskers. *Old. Bitter. Malevolent. It clings to the room like cobwebs.*

Rosa sneezed and said, *No natural oils. Pure chemicals.*

Somehow Laurie doubted that, but she told Skye what the animals were saying.

"So, they all sense it," Skye murmured.

Thistle sat back and wrapped his tail around his paws. *If you intend to follow this scent, take the canines. I'll monitor from here. Someone must protect the premises.*

Like you stopped the thief the first time? Rosa asked sarcastically. But Thistle only flicked his tail.

Laurie chuckled. "A cat-and-dog magical task force. This could be fun."

Fun, Thistle repeated, arching an eyebrow, *is a mortal word for chaos.*

Laurie translated and Skye shook her head, but her lips curved into a smile. "Thank you, all of you."

Rosa's tail wagged. Thistle gave a dignified blink. Ashe sat, red tongue lolling, ignoring the snipping. And for a brief moment, witch, animal whisperer, dogs, and cat stood united—guardians of Star, Stone & Flower and the mystery that had just begun to unfold.

Laurie glanced at her watch. "Oops. I've got to run. John asked me to come to the city council meeting."

"I'll walk you out." Dark gray clouds promised more rain. Even a bit of snow. Skye pulled her coat tighter, watching her breath cloud in the air. "Thanks for coming. This has shaken me."

"We'll find him," Laurie said. "We always figure things out."

The knot in Skye's stomach loosened just a bit. All along the street, twinkle lights shimmered on rain-damp lampposts, their reflections glimmering like faerie fire on the wet pavement. Somewhere nearby, a busker played a soft, minor-key version of "Carol of the Bells."

Laurie opened her car door. She wished she'd gotten a chance to see this mystical crystal skull. She wondered what he looked like.

CHAPTER
SEVEN

M arco Bellini's doorbell chimed a soft, musical tone. A faint voice called, "It's open," and Skye, Laurie, and Dana all stepped into his home, Rosa on their heels. The morning light fractured through a hundred crystal surfaces, splashing rainbows across the whitewashed walls. The air was warm with sandalwood and the faint tang of ozone—the scent of freshly cleared energy.

"Mr. Bellini?" Skye called softly.

A man in his late sixties stood beside a glass display case filled with every shade of quartz and gemstone. Skye counted at least five crystal skulls at first glance—clear, smoky, rose quartz, and one deep amethyst that made her palms tingle. The owner of this opulent display moved forward, sleeves rolled, a magnifying lens still in one hand. His dark hair, graying at the temples, caught the prisms of light.

"Ah—Skye Yarrow, Laurie Olson, and Dana Preston, yes? I've heard of your family, Ms. Yarrow."

Skye tried to hide her surprise. "Please, call me Skye."

"You may call me Marco." He bent, offering the back of his hand for Rosa to sniff. "And who is this charming creature?"

"Rosa, my Havanese," Laurie said.

Marco studied Laurie for a beat, amusement in his eyes. "Ah—you're an animal communicator."

Laurie blinked. "Uh...yes. How did you guess?"

He tilted his head toward Rosa, chuckling. "She told me, of course." His voice held the smooth resonance of a seasoned lecturer who was perfectly at ease with mysteries. "Please, sit."

They settled onto a sofa, Dana in a bentwood rocker across from a well-worn armchair that clearly belonged to their host.

"What brings you talented women to my corner of the city?"

Skye exchanged a glance with her friends, then drew a breath. "It's about a crystal. A crystal skull."

Marco's gaze sharpened. "You have one?"

"We did," Skye said, her voice tightening. "But he's been stolen."

Marco glanced at Rosa and chuckled softly.

Skye frowned. "What?"

"The dog tells her mistress I didn't steal your skull," he said mildly.

Laurie's cheeks pinked. "Sorry she suspected you."

"I appreciate a thorough detective." Marco scratched Rosa's silky head.

The little Havanese accepted the attention like a queen being greeted by a loyal subject, then trotted off to recon the kitchen.

"When the skull arrived," Skye continued, "I was...apprehensive. But he felt peaceful. Loving, even. Then he spoke to me. He said his name is Anuun."

Dana did a double take. "You never told us that."

The magnifying lens slipped from Marco's fingers and landed with a soft thud on the maroon carpet. "Anuun," he repeated, tasting the name like a long-lost note. "Describe him, please."

Skye's hands moved as if shaping the air. "Clear quartz with a milky white cap near the crown—like a veil of frost. Perfectly carved. Gentle, warm. When you touch him, it feels like he's...connecting."

Marco's eyes widened, and for a heartbeat the room's light seemed to gather about him. "It has a white cap?" His voice dropped. "I've been looking for that skull for thirty years."

Rosa returned and curled at Marco's feet.

"You know it?" Laurie asked.

He nodded, gesturing to a low table crowded with smaller skulls. His fingers brushed a rose quartz piece that glowed faintly in response. "Legend says Anuun is among the purest ever carved. A healing skull, untainted by the darker rites that affected others. Its frequency aligns with unity, higher consciousness, regeneration. Those who meditate with it report visions—or a deep, steady knowing. It amplifies what is pure in the heart—" he glanced at them "—and reveals what is not."

"Why would anyone steal it?" Laurie asked.

"Because purity is power," Marco said, settling into his chair. "Magnified intention can heal—or control. In the wrong hands..." He left the sentence to finish itself.

Skye swallowed. "So, he could be hurt by whoever stole him."

"Yes, and if this is the skull I think it is," he said gently, "you've stepped into a very old struggle."

He rose with a soft sigh and crossed to a tall cabinet crowded with rare stones and weathered artifacts. From a locked drawer he withdrew a folio wrapped in indigo silk. "A gift from a Mayan elder near Palenque. He said it was a copy of a codex lost when the Spanish burned the libraries."

They leaned in as he untied the cords. Faded glyphs, circular diagrams, and meticulous sketches of crystal skulls filled the parchment—each crowned with elemental symbols.

"This is exquisite," Dana breathed.

"The Thirteen," Marco murmured. "Legends say there were thirteen original skulls, carved before recorded history, each attuned to a facet of consciousness. Together, they amplify human awareness—bridging seen and unseen worlds."

"Like a network?" Skye asked.

"Exactly. I suspect there are circles of thirteen tied to sacred sites —twelve human-sized skulls around a larger master. Those master skulls formed a crystalline web across the planet." He traced rings on the page. "Glastonbury. Giza. Lake Titicaca. Sedona. Kailash. Maunakea...and others." He tapped near the Yucatán. "Anuun was called the Heart—the one to restore harmony when the others fell quiet."

"Harmony to what?" Dana asked.

"To Gaia herself," Marco said. "When humanity turned from Earth's natural rhythms, many circles went dormant. But Anuun remained...watching."

"So, whoever took him—" Laurie began.

"Is no common thief," Marco finished, closing the folio. "They'll learn what he is—if they don't already. Once Anuun is bound to someone's intent, his resonance shifts to serve it."

A hush fell. Even the rainbow light seemed to dim, listening.

"Can we rescue him?" Skye asked.

"Perhaps," Marco said, studying her. "If you can hear him, you're already part of his song. But tread carefully."

"Because others might be listening," Laurie said.

He nodded. "Not all who seek the skulls do so for healing."

Rosa whined softly. Marco stooped to stroke her head. "And our little ally here," he smiled, "has already taken the thief's scent. Good work."

Rosa's tail thumped. "Obviously," Laurie translated dryly.

Marco moved to a sideboard dotted with crystal spheres and points. "There's one way to see if Anuun is still...singing." He set a clear quartz pyramid, a smoky citrine, and a pale aquamarine sphere upon a round obsidian mirror, forming a small triangle. Closing his eyes, he hummed a low, steady tone.

Rosa tipped her chin and offered a respectful, muted howl. The air shifted. Curtains stirred though no window was open. Light pulsed through the crystals in time with his voice. Skye felt it then—an answering thrum beneath her sternum, ancient and intimate.

Marco opened his eyes. "There. Do you feel it?"

"Yes," Skye whispered.

"You're attuned," Marco said softly. "Not just sensitive. You work with energy—herbs, stone, air?"

Laurie grinned. "You've got her pegged. Skye owns Star, Stone & Flower—the witchy shop in the U District."

"Ah," Marco said, eyes lighting. "That explains the shift in resonance when you walked in. You're no ordinary visitor, Signora Yarrow."

Skye flushed but held his gaze. "So, what does it mean—that I can sense him?"

"It means," Marco said, lowering his voice, "that Anuun is still himself. He's reaching for his keeper."

"Keeper?"

"Why you, of course."

Skye blinked, startled, but deep down she knew it was true.

He turned back to the crystals, where faint light flickered between the points like tiny lightning. "His signal is faint, confused. Whoever took him is masking his resonance—like one bell hidden among a thousand echoes."

"Can you trace it?" Dana asked.

"Not today. The energy must settle first. But Anuun isn't gone. His vibration is tethered to yours, Skye. When the time is right, he'll call again."

The shimmer faded into quiet.

"Marco," Skye said softly, "you've studied these skulls for decades. Who else knows about Anuun? Who might have taken him?"

He sighed and shook his head.

Dana looked at him carefully. "You do have ideas, though."

Marco huffed out a breath, then stood and walked toward the window, staring out at the garden where moonlight caught the quartz steppingstones like frozen stars. "There are three names that come to mind. None of them good."

He returned to his seat and picked up a smoky skull, letting it glow in his palm. "First, Celeste Ardolf. She is on what could loosely be called the crystal skull circuit. She runs workshops and lectures about the history of the skulls. She knows only the surface stories that circulate. Claims hers came from Atlantis and carries the codes for remaking the planet."

Laurie's forehead wrinkled. "What does that mean?"

"Crystals, particularly quartz, are essential in electronics for their piezoelectric properties, which allow them to generate and respond to electrical signals with precise, stable vibrations. This makes them the core component of crystal oscillators, which act as highly accurate timing sources and frequency references for devices like computers, smartphones, radios, and clocks. They are used to synchronize operations, ensure accurate data transmission, and stabilize frequencies for reliable performance."

Skye looked at her friends and saw surprise on their faces. She turned to Marco. "Seriously?"

He nodded. "It's true. They channel and some say store energy. It's believed in some circles that information can be saved in the gaps in the crystalline structure of the stone. The brain can 'read,'" he put the word in air quotes, "piezoelectric energy and download this information."

"Pfft," Dana said in disbelief.

Marco shrugged. "Legend states these ancient artifacts store vast knowledge that humans can access. Ardolf claims they are encoded with the matrixes of life itself." He chuckled. "That's a little above my pay grade, but she spouts off things she's heard or read with little or no understanding."

"So, if she took Anuun?" Skye prompted.

"Ardolf does private readings and healings with people where she channels, or pretends to channel, what her skull tells her. She claims the piece is ancient, but I know who carved it five years ago. It's a modern skull." He said this with some heat.

"Anyway, when she opens herself up like this, what she doesn't realize is that any entity can use her as a tool."

Dana snorted.

Marco fixed her with a look. "She doesn't believe this either, but that's what makes her dangerous. If she has Anuun, negative forces could use her to corrupt his purity."

"Oh, I know there are spirits," Dana said.

"She sees ghosts," Laurie explained.

Marco looked surprised, but Dana answered Laurie back. "I hope I'm done seeing them."

Marco studied her, his long index finger on his chin. "Hmm, I don't think so."

Before Dana could object, Skye pulled them back on track. "You said there were three suspects."

Marco gave Skye a nod. He lifted a small fluorite skull from a nearby shelf and let the light catch its facets. "Second," he said, "is Dr. Victor Salazar. We worked together years ago on a dig near Palenque—back when he still believed in peer review."

"He's gone off the rails?" Skye felt a stab of sympathy for their host.

He sighed, half fond, half weary. "Victor now claims the skulls are divine vessels—avatars of celestial beings trapped in stone."

"Avatars like the movie?" Laurie covered a grin.

This pulled a laugh from Marco. "Like divine beings from the Vedic stories. I'm told he's been searching for 'the pure one,' the skull untouched by the blood sacrifices the Aztec performed. That can only mean Anuun. Salazar would steal Anuun not for money, but to *activate* it."

"Seems to me Anuun is activated already," Skye said.

Laurie glanced at her. "That sounds like the kind of person who could do real harm without meaning to."

Marco nodded grimly. "Victor never understood restraint."

He set down the fluorite skull and selected a darker one. "And finally, Adrian Vale—wealthy collector, operates under the pretense of funding archaeological recovery. In truth, he's built a private museum for himself, objects that hum with power. He offered me a fortune for one of my skulls last year. When I refused, someone broke into my storeroom two weeks later."

"Did they steal it?"

Marco shook his head. "I'd moved it already, so no. I suspected he'd pull off some stunt like that."

Skye's eyes darkened. "My family knows about Adrian Vale," she murmured. "He'd put Anuun on a pedestal and keep him under lock and key."

Laurie looked between them. "Looks like we've got a New Age con artist, an obsessed archaeologist, and a collector. All after the same artifact."

"Each for different reasons," Marco said. "Power, spiritual knowledge, ostentation. But none of them understand what they're playing with."

For a long moment, nobody spoke. Then Marco crossed to a smaller cabinet near the far wall—an antique apothecary chest lined with drawers labeled in Latin.

He opened one and withdrew a pouch of soft gray suede. "You'll need protection," he said quietly.

He poured a few stones into his palm: a quartz shard veined with gold and a small disc of carved obsidian. "This quartz is from Teotihuacán—it once stood in a temple wall. The obsidian grounds it. Keep them together, close to your skin."

"Thank you." Skye accepted them, feeling their warmth. "You think one of them might already be trying to track us?"

Marco's gaze was steady. "Not might. The moment you touched Anuun, you became visible to anyone who knows how to look."

"They sound more quirky than dangerous," Dana said.

"Quirky, yes, but don't underestimate the havoc they could cause.

"None of you are defenseless," he said softly. "The skull chose Skye for a reason. Its frequency matches her intent—and that cannot be feigned."

He turned back to the chest, choosing more stones. "For you, Laurie—an aquamarine and obsidian. The sea is in you."

Laurie smiled. "My partner and I work on ocean restoration."

"Then this will strengthen that bond." He tucked the stones into a silver pouch.

"For our brilliant lawyer," he said, turning to Dana.

"How did you know?"

"I followed Senator Whitmore's revelations closely. You're working with her, am I right?"

Dana nodded.

"A citrine for clarity and obsidian for grounding." He paused, studying her through squinted eyes. He added a rose-pink stone veined with white. "And rhodochrosite—for healing the heart."

Dana's eyes shimmered. "Thank you."

Marco nodded. "These stones will protect and guide you while the search unfolds. And remember, all of you—you're not alone in this. The stones listen."

He gave them a gentle bow. "Call if you need me."

They thanked Marco profusely for his gifts and the knowledge he'd shared with them. Then stepped into the bright Seattle daylight, clutching their new talismans. The air smelled of cedar and fresh rain.

"Well," Laurie said, exhaling. "That was...enlightening."

Skye smiled faintly. "And a little terrifying."

"He's the real deal," Dana said.

Skye glanced back at Marco's window, where sunlight glinted like an eye. "I can still feel Anuun. Faint—but there."

They walked toward their cars, the hum of city life rising around them. Beneath it all, Skye felt the pulse again—slow and luminous, like a heartbeat of light.

"He's trying to find his way home," she murmured.

Laurie turned her keys. "We'll be listening."

As they drove away, sunlight scattered tiny rainbows across Skye's dashboard—a quiet reminder that somewhere, the crystal skull still shimmered, waiting to be found.

CHAPTER
EIGHT

Dana started her SUV and eased out into traffic, the electric engine barely silent beneath the drizzle tapping her windshield. "Bướm, call Maxwell."

She'd named her voice command the Vietnamese word for *butterfly* because no one was likely to say it accidentally. Her kids thought it was hilarious and had nearly unleashed chaos one night just by whispering it back and forth like a spell.

The call connected and—after a single ring—the line went eerily silent, as if the world on Maxwell's end had been vacuum-sealed.

Dana snorted. "You're such a drama queen," she muttered, shifting her grip on the wheel. Maxwell did love his spy theatrics almost as much as he loved lecturing people about them. "I've got a situation."

"You always have a situation," he replied, his voice low and dry, carrying that familiar half-annoyed, half-amused lilt. She could practically hear him rolling his eyes.

"I've got three names for you. Ready?"

"Is your line secure?"

Dana merged into a slower lane as a city bus groaned past,

kicking up fine spray from the wet pavement. "You installed that... thingy on my cell."

"Thingy?" he echoed, affronted. "You mean the impregnable quantum-shield firewall I uploaded for you?"

She bit back a laugh. "Yeah, that thingy."

Maxwell exhaled one of his trademark exaggerated sighs, the kind that suggested he was pinching the bridge of his nose. "You can't text like a normal person?"

"I'm driving."

"You can talk and it'll type, you know. It's not the twentieth century anymore."

"I am not that old, "she said, turning onto a narrower street lined with moss-darkened brick buildings and rain-glossed evergreens. "I'll send the names—plus other info—when I get home. Are you available today?"

Maxwell chuckled, the warm, smug kind that meant he knew he'd gotten under her skin. "I love riling you up. It's so easy."

"You're worse than my teenagers," she said, though the warmth in her tone softened the words. A neon coffee sign reflected in her windshield like a flickering rune.

"Tell me the basics."

As she described the theft, the crystal skull, and the suspects, the city slid by in watery motion—old craftsman bungalows, modern glass boxes, corner cafes with fogged windows, and the distant shimmer of the Sound where a lone shaft of sunlight broke through the cloud cover like a blessing.

"You guys are always into some wild stuff," he murmured, distracted. Dana could practically picture him now: hunched over his array of glowing monitors, screens reflecting in his glasses, fingers already dancing at manic speed.

"You're one to talk," she said.

"Send me what you've got when you get home. I don't want you crashing into anybody while you're driving," Maxwell teased.

"Will do."

She ended the call, exhaled, and let the quiet settle. Lake Union opened to her right, the slate-gray water flecked with whitecaps from the wind. Seaplanes bobbed against their moorings, and the Space Needle loomed ghostlike through the mist.

She let herself breathe—Seattle's weather always did its best to wash everything clean—but the weight in her chest stayed put. Marcos was quite a character and he knew a great deal about metaphysical history, a world she was starting to take more seriously. She glanced at her cell phone, wondering about the crystal inside.

She reached Capitol Hill, where the streets narrowed and the old maples dripped from the morning rain. Ahead, the cathedral's spires cut into a pewter sky, a faint light glimmering behind them like a promise—or a warning. Dana tightened her grip on the wheel. She was glad there were no ghosts involved this time, then winced, hoping she hadn't jinxed herself. She straightened her shoulders. Whatever waited for them next, she'd be ready.

Skye's family sat around the long oak dining table, the air still fragrant with basil and lemon from the angel hair pasta Fíona had made for supper. Candles burned low in the center, their wax pooling in soft golden puddles, and the last of the red wine gleamed in half-empty glasses. Beyond the window, the night pressed close, fog curling off the orchard like a living thing.

"I can't believe somebody got into the store." Her father shook his head, his weathered hands curling around his glass. The lines at the corners of his eyes deepened, shadowed by worry.

Jade nodded. "Nothing was broken. The lock on the back door was intact. The safe open."

"What does that mean? A professional? Somebody who knew the place?" Cormac wondered, his brows knit tight.

Grandmother Brigid toyed with her fork, her silver hair gleaming in the candlelight. "Sounds more like somebody with magical abilities to me."

"I'm inclined to think it's one of Marco's suspects. At least, I'd like to check them out first." Skye pushed her plate away. The fragrant pasta—usually a favorite—sat unfinished, her stomach tight with unease.

Her mother started to speak, perhaps to chide her for wasting food, but then sighed softly and reached across to touch Skye's hand. "Seems you got attached to this rock."

"I've never heard of such a thing," Grandmother Brigid said, tightening her shawl around her shoulders as if warding off a chill.

"I know, Grandma. I felt the same when I first saw it was a skull, but he's not scary at all. Just the opposite," Skye said gently.

Sorcha leaned forward, her eyes bright. "He's loving and peaceful. Helps me feel all Zen even when things get chaotic in the store."

"I remember how hectic it gets this time of year," Fíona said with a knowing smile. "The Yule rush never did wait for anyone's nerves to settle."

Grandmother Brigid tsked in disapproval. "I'm not so sure about talking to skulls."

Cormac turned toward his brother's wife. "Marisol, you know anything about these things?"

Marisol set down her wineglass, the garnet liquid catching the candlelight. "Oh, yes," she said thoughtfully. "In Mexico, crystal skulls are part of our old traditions. The ancient ones, from before the Spanish came." Her dark eyes glimmered with memory. "They say each skull holds the wisdom of an ancestor or a spirit teacher."

Salazar must have gotten his idea from this legend, Skye thought.

"The Maya and the Aztec used them in ceremonies—some for healing, others for guidance. They believed the skulls could speak—through visions, dreams, or a kind of inner knowing."

The family listened in silence as her voice softened. "People bring them to altars during Día de los Muertos. Not because they worship them, but because they honor what they represent—the bridge between the living and the spirit world. If this one came to you, Skye, it's because you're ready for your next step."

A hush settled over the table. Even Brigid's skeptical frown eased as if the idea, strange as it was, carried a quiet resonance. Outside, the wind sighed through the pines like a distant echo of something ancient and knowing.

Grandmother Brigid was the first to move. She adjusted her shawl again, her silver bangles catching the candlelight. "Thank you, Marisol," she said warmly. "It's a blessing to hear the old ways honored so beautifully. We sometimes forget how many paths lead to the same mystery."

Her gaze settled on Skye, soft and full of understanding. "It sounds to me like this Anuun carries wisdom meant for you, lass. Best to listen with both your heart and your magic."

Emotion welled unexpectedly in Skye's chest. Her grandmother's path, so ancient and steady, had always been her anchor. "I will, Grandma," she said quietly. "I promise."

Jade squeezed Skye's knee beneath the table, her grounding presence steady as ever. "If these skulls connect to ancestors," she said to Marisol, "then maybe Anuun—" she glanced at Skye "—was meant to help you uncover something. Or protect something."

Marisol nodded slowly. "Perhaps both. In my grandmother's village, they say skulls pick their own keepers. Spirits have their own timing and their own reasons."

"That's an interesting idea," Cormac muttered, but he studied Skye with some unease.

Sorcha leaned forward, her curls bouncing. "So, you agree with what Marco told Skye. That the skull chose her?"

Marisol smiled. "Sí, niña. The relic chooses its keeper, not the other way around."

A shiver ran down Skye's spine—half wonder, half fear. "That's exactly what Marco said," she whispered, "That he would call out to me."

The candle flames fluttered just then, bending toward her as though in answer.

Grandmother Brigid and Fíona glanced at each other, then gave a decisive nod. "We'll do a protection spell."

Skye lifted her suede pouch, the faint scent of cedar and sage rising from it. "Marco already gave me this for protection."

Grandmother Brigid leaned over and patted her head like she was still eight. "That's nice, dear, but we'll put a stronger layer around you."

"And your friends," Fíona added, her tone brisk but kind. "Will they be involved in this?"

"Yes. Laurie's been with me at every step, and Dana came with us to see the Dean of Crystal Skulls." Skye waved her pouch lightly when she said this. "Rosa confirmed he was not the thief."

"Then we'll include them and the little pooch."

"Dana's coming over tomorrow. She's got her hacker checking out the three suspects Marco mentioned, plus anything else he can find."

A soft snort came from the far end of the table. "I can't say I'd be trustin' those computer contraptions," Grandmother Moira said. Her voice was roughened by age and a touch of laughter. "We'll be addin' a location spell for this crystal that's come to ye. Best not leave it to machines."

"Good idea," Jade said, smiling toward her.

Moira nodded, satisfied. "Iona, lass, check the grimoires for anythin' about this stone head."

"Yes, ma'am. And for location spells?"

"I think we've got that handled, but—" she waved her hand, the motion graceful despite her gnarled fingers "—as ye wish. Ye might learn a thing or two."

"I'll get right on it."

Jade rose to help clear the table while Fíona brought over gingerbread and pumpkin loaves, breaking up the family conference. The air filled with the cozy scent of spice and molasses. Jade fetched a stack of smaller plates and dessert forks as Fíona lifted her bread knife like a queen with her scepter.

"Who wants what?" she asked, grinning.

Everyone called out their orders, voices overlapping with laughter, and Jade added a dollop of cream for those who asked. Between bites, the talk turned to ordinary family chatter and a touch of gossip —how the businesses were going, who'd gotten into trouble at school, who'd finally repaired the hay loft after five years of threatening to do it.

Skye sat back, watching the scene through the soft haze of candlelight, grateful for her clan—loud, loving, a bit much at times, but hers. Jade bumped her shoulder as she sat down with a slice of gingerbread smothered in cream.

Skye raised an eyebrow at the high pile, and Jade grinned. "It's almost Solstice," she said.

Skye laughed softly. "Guess that's reason enough."

Outside, the wind sighed through the orchard again, as if echoing the family's magic gathering quietly in the room.

CHAPTER
NINE

The posse, as John had christened the three friends, gathered in the reading room at the back of Star, Stone & Flower on Solstice morning. The air was rich with the scent of incense, wrapping paper, and cardboard. The faint smell of evergreen boughs and the hum of customer's voices drifted in from the front.

Dana dropped her bag on the table and pulled out her laptop. "You would not believe Seattle traffic today. Half the city decided to drive like Mercury's in retrograde."

"We have Wi-Fi, you know," Skye said, watching her friend plug in a small black device.

"Yeah, but Maxwell gave me this little beauty." Dana tapped it proudly. "Hot sauce security—his words, not mine. It's unhackable, untraceable, and probably singes the eyebrows off anyone who tries to snoop."

"Nothing like mild arson for data protection." Laurie grabbed a stool next her, and Rosa went off to make her rounds, nosing into every corner. Wild Rose jumped to a high perch to watch.

"And—" Dana held up an index finger "—he also managed to

slip trackers on our suspects' phones—well, two out of three. One of them's running dark."

Skye leaned in. "Which one?"

"Vale," Dana said. "Rich guy's got a talent for vanishing. Probably keeps his phone in a lead-lined case between his cashmere socks."

Before anyone could reply, Sorcha swept in like a caffeine fairy, balancing a tray of drinks and muffins. "Mochas, lattes, and eggnog chai from Northbean—plus goodies from the bakery. Gluten-free for you, Dana." She set them down with a grin.

"Bless you," Laurie murmured, wrapping her hands around her cup like it was holy water for the under-caffeinated.

Sorcha brushed her hands together after she distributed everything. "Solstice day—brace yourselves, it's going to be nuts in here."

"Thanks, sweetie," Skye said. "Mom's already in, reorganizing the candle display by planetary alignment."

"Yeah," Sorcha muttered, raising an eyebrow. "She's *helping*."

Skye sputtered a laugh. "She still thinks this is her shop. A few more people are coming in—some to work here, some at the apothecary. That should dilute her fussing a bit."

Sorcha bounced off and Dana snapped back into command mode. "Right. Maxwell's been digging. And he found a *lot*. Ready?"

"Ready as caffeine allows," Skye said.

Dana swiveled the laptop around. "We checked out Marco's suspects. First up, Dr. Celeste Ardolf. Owns a gem and mineral shop in town. Just flew back from the Yucatán Peninsula. She was a speaker on some cruise featuring crystal skulls and visiting Mayan sites."

"There were enough people to fill one of those big boats?" Laurie asked.

"Probably not a giant one," Dana said, "but Maxwell checked into it and quite a lot of people are following this crystal skull craze."

"We've been getting requests for them in the store," Skye said. "I didn't want to carry them at first. Thought people were into dark magic and we don't encourage that sort of thing. But now..."

"Now we know they can be a positive force," Laurie finished for her.

Dana tapped a key on her computer and another picture swam to life. "Dr. Victor Salazar. Former archaeology professor, now self-proclaimed 'independent researcher.' Translation: fired for stealing museum artifacts. Maxwell says now he travels to Central America with other crystal skull dealers. He has a theory about how they sneak in the ancient skulls they've dug up at archaeological sites."

"How?" Laurie asked, setting down her half empty chai.

"They mix them in with the modern ones they ordered from local carvers. It's illegal, of course."

A loud hiss sounded from the back of the store near the office followed by an unhappy yip.

That's my food. Laurie heard a feline voice and recognized Wild Rose.

But you didn't eat it all. I eat all my food, Rosa answered.

Laurie felt the little dog going for another bite. "Rosa, no."

Wild Rose responded with a growl of protest. A sharp yelp sounded and Rosa thundered back to safety, ducking beneath Laurie's legs.

Rosa, are you hungry? You had a big breakfast, Laurie asked.

There was food just sitting there. Going to waste, she explained.

Laurie chuckled and bent down to inspect the little Havanese for any wounds. She found a small, red scratch on her nose. *Does this hurt?*

Rosa gave her a sad look. *Her claws are sharp.*

Laurie took a wet wipe from her purse—she didn't have kids, but dogs made as many messes, it seemed—and cleaned the nick. *Better now?*

Thank you.

Laurie looked up to find the rest of the posse watching her.

Skye glanced down at Rosa. "Trying to eat the cats' food?"

Rosa only sniffed in answer, then circled three times beneath Laurie's stool, and laid down, tucking her nose beneath her paw.

Used to the interruptions from her kids, Dana started right up where she'd left off. "Next, Adrian Vale. Wealthy collector of occult objects. Rumor has it he bankrolls the underground artifact trade in L.A. among other places. And guess who he's related to?"

Skye's stomach dropped. "Don't say it."

"Sir Reginald Fairfax." Dana showed them a picture of him on the web. "Your very own posh shop visitor. The man who Skye said practically oozed old money and cologne when he came sniffing around for crystal skulls."

Laurie groaned. "Of course he's involved. And plotting something shady."

"I thought he was just eccentric," Skye said, "but he had this... courtly thing going on. Like he stepped out of a BBC mystery."

"Yeah," Dana said. "A BBC *villain* special."

Skye crossed her arms. "Any other suspects."

"Maxwell scoured your security feeds. He couldn't find any identifying details of the thief," Dana said. "Even Maxwell couldn't get anything from the ghostly face Cillian saw."

Rosa lifted her head. *I know what he smells like.*

Laurie repeated this for the group.

"You're sure it's a man?" Dana asked. "Because my talented hacker did find this woman." She turned the screen to show an image of a woman in a black velvet, floor length gown, a matching hood pulled over her head and forehead, almost obscuring her face.

"Great Goddess, I remember her. She asked for a crystal bust. When I told her we didn't have any crystals for sale the size she was looking for, she didn't believe me."

"She could have come back to steal Anuun," Laurie said.

"Refused to give me her name. Acted like I'd use it in some spell to cause her harm," Skye said. "Thistle jumped down on the counter and hissed at her."

The little dog lifted her head. *Did she try to take his food?*

Laurie stifled a laugh. *I don't think so.*

Rosa put her head back down on her paw. *It was a man who took the ball of light.*

Laurie smiled at Rosa's description of Anuun. "My dog is sure the thief is male,"

"She could have hired a man to take it for her. Or maybe her partner or a member of her coven broke in," Dana pointed out.

"Maybe." Laurie drew out the word to suggest she doubted this.

"Maxwell discovered her name," Dana said, "and much more." She sat back, arms crossed.

They both stared at her. "Are you going to tell us?"

"Ravenna Crowhurst. Real name Jane Smith."

Laurie burst out laughing. Both Dana and Skye shook their heads in disbelief.

She shrugged. "I mean, what a bland name. No wonder she wanted to have a fancy alias."

"Actually, that's her spirit name. She's high priestess of a local coven. Teaches third grade at Laurelhurst Elementary."

Skye's jaw dropped. "No way."

"Way," Dana said, imitating her teenagers.

Skye shook her head. "That's the last thing I would have imagined."

"How did she know about Anuun, then?"

"Maxwell is trying to find out. He's checking out all the members of her coven, but these people are more secretive than CIA assets. He's uncovered two who are more white bread than—" Dana paused "—well, white bread. One's a bank clerk, the other works retail at The Daily Thread."

"Is she well connected in the pagan community? Maybe she heard about him from somebody else?" Skye asked.

"Could be. Thing is," Dana stabbed the air with her finger. "Maxwell doesn't think she stole Anuun. He traced her phone and she stayed home that night—"

"She could have left it," Laurie objected.

"—and the bank clerk's phone was also in her apartment," Dana finished saying. "Those two were probably busy doing other things the night of the theft."

"Ooh la la." Skye waggled her eyebrows.

Laurie rolled her eyes. "Do we need more coffee in here?"

Dana took charge again. "We have three strong suspects. And the BBC villain guy is related to one of them."

"Sir Reginald, yes. I think we can count him in with Adrian Vale. Then we have Victor Salazar and Celeste Ardolf." Dana ticked them off on her fingers. "Maxwell's tracking their locations as best he can. Ardolf's seeing clients, Salazar checked into a downtown hotel under a fake name, and Vale's at his mansion."

Laurie sighed. "All of them might be colluding, right at solstice."

"Yup. Big energy window, rare celestial alignment—take your pick," Skye said. "Whatever they're planning, it's happening soon."

Dana snapped her fingers. "That reminds me. Maxwell discovered that Celeste always holds a public ritual—more of a party, really —in Volunteer Park the night after solstice."

"That won't be it, but somebody should go. See what she's up to," Skye said.

From under Laurie's chair came a soft rumble. Rosa lifted her head, her eyes gleaming like polished amber. *They're in cahoots*, she said.

Laurie glanced down. "Rosa, sweetheart, you've been listening?"

Of course, Rosa told Laurie. *The tall one—the thief with the burned lightning smell—I could follow that scent through a thunderstorm.*

Laurie translated and Dana smiled. "It still amazes me that she talks."

I sass, Rosa said

Laurie laughed.

"What did she say?" Dana asked.

When Laurie told them, Skye snorted. "Okay, listen up, team Sass and Sauce. Dana, you and Maxwell keep digging—financials, travel, rentals, hidden temples, anything shady. Laurie, reach out to your academic contacts, see if anyone's heard of Salazar. I'll ask my family about Ardolf and her coven. Somebody's bound to know something."

Dana nodded. "Good. If Maxwell finds anything, I'll text—encrypted, obviously."

Laurie raised her coffee cup. "To the Sisterhood of Supernatural Snoops."

Skye clinked hers against it. "Long may we sass."

Rosa gave a little bark. *And sniff.*

"Ritual starts around six. You're all coming, right?"

"Wouldn't miss it," Laurie said.

"We'll be there early," Dana said. "The kids want to help prepare."

The laughter drifted up into the rafters, light and warm against the gray Seattle morning. But as it faded, Laurie caught a faint shimmer of light spilling from beneath the back-room door—just a flicker, like crystal catching the sun where no sun should reach.

THE WINTER AFTERNOON glowed gold over Red Fox Farm, the low sun catching on frost-rimmed fences and the distant shimmer of the orchard. Indoors, the house bustled—someone was always carrying a tray of cookies through the hallway, stockings were being hung, and the scent of warm cider and rosemary bread drifted from the kitchen. The sun set at half past four and the ritual was scheduled for around eight.

Inside, the kitchen smelled of cinnamon and mulled cider. The scents of fish and vegetables and some delicious soup competed. Sprigs of cedar and holly hung from the beams, and a great wreath of evergreens lay half-finished on a worktable just inside the living room.

"Now you'd best clean up after yerselves," Grandma Moira fussed. "I'll not be sweeping up needles all winter."

"Yes, ma'am," rose from two teens bent over the wreath.

Hoa, Dana's daughter, immediately abandoned her mother as soon as they arrived, rushing to help decorate the towering Balsam fir standing proud in front of the bay window. Siobhán supervised. "Spread out the ornaments. Small ones on top."

Laurie and John came in through the mudroom, shaking off their coats. Rosa trotted in at Laurie's heels, tail wagging, then gave a hopeful sniff toward the plate of gingerbread cookies cooling on the counter.

Grandmother Moira shook her finger at her. "They be too hot fer ye, little one."

Laurie looked back to find Oliver, her parents' boxer, standing stock still in the doorway while Ashe and Taran arrived and sniffed the boxer from stem to stern. Laurie's parents had taken off for a holiday trip and she was taking care of their pets.

Rosa ran over to them. *He's my pack mate,* she explained. With a sharp bark, Taran turned and took off toward the woods. The other dogs followed.

"Don't roll in anything," Laurie and Skye shouted at the same time.

Cormac rubbed his hands on his apron. "Not much chance of that."

Laurie greeted Fíona and Cormac who were baking more cookies and what looked like fruitcake. Did people still eat that stuff?

"Welcome. You can taste some soon, but we're saving most for after the ritual," Fíona said.

"Sounds great." Laurie set a six-pack of Christmas beer on the table, thinking it was a meager offering. She followed John into what Minh had christened the war room during their previous investigation. There they found Maxwell Briggs who had put in a rare appearance. He sat before a laptop that glowed with code, fingers flying, the blue light reflecting in his glasses. He looked like a hacker elf who'd been put to work in Santa's workshop.

Minh leaned against the wall behind him, sipping cider and following his every key stroke. Jade was there too, still in her dark uniform trousers but with her jacket draped over a chair, her badge tucked away. She'd just finished a shift and had come straight from Seattle. Her calm, steady presence seemed to anchor the room.

Dana sat at the long table near the fireplace. A cheerful fire crackled inside. It seemed there were fireplaces everywhere in this old farmhouse. A glass of white wine sat in front of her and a gingerbread cookie was halfway to her mouth. Laurie screwed up her mouth in distaste. Those didn't even go together. And how had she scored a cookie so fast?

"Any news?" John asked Maxwell.

The hacker spun around in his chair, his mismatched socks and over-caffeinated grin both on full display.

The farmhouse shuddered slightly as someone upstairs stomped —probably one of Skye's cousins hauling boxes of decorations down for the upcoming ritual. The momentary vibration made the holly bells on the living room mantle jingle.

"Okay," he muttered, not looking up. "I've got updates. And several new questions. Also, I need a Christmas ale."

Dana crossed her arms. "Just give us the important parts."

Hoa, halfway down the hall, called, "Hurry! Aunt Siobhán says the best ornaments get hung before sunset!"

Minh—now eighteen and full of restless energy—told her. "We'll help with the tree as soon as we're finished."

Laurie grabbed a beer from the kitchen—maybe it had been a good choice after all—and set it next to the hacker. Skye swept through with a tray of bright citrus candles. "Tell us everything— quickly. I have to charge the torches before the ritual."

Maxwell clicked open the first file titled **Celeste Ardolf — New Age con artist, but mostly clueless**

Dana chuckled at the label.

The hacker cleared his throat. "I take it Dana has filled you in on the basics."

Murmurs of agreement greeted this statement.

"Celeste has been texting someone about an 'energetic treasure' that slipped through her fingers. And that someone's IP leads to a VPN I can't crack yet."

Skye frowned. "We definitely need to check her out."

"And here's your chance." Maxwell grabbed the beer and took a long swallow. "Celeste is giving a workshop tomorrow night at her shop called *Crystal Resonance & Galactic Unity*."

Skye let out a dramatic sigh worthy of a stage production. "Well... so much for a cozy evening by the fire with my sweetie." She glanced at Dana and Laurie, brows raised in a please-don't-make-me-do-this-alone sort of plea.

Dana groaned but lifted a hand in surrender. "Fine. We'll go. Both of us."

Laurie blinked between them. Her shoulders slumped. "If you need us both, I'm in."

"Not so fast on that," Maxwell said and clicked open a second file. It bore the title **Dr. Victor Salazar — Archaeologist obsessed with 'the pure one'**

He flipped to a photo of a thin man with desert-scorched skin and intense eyes. "Salazar's last two research papers were about purity in sacred objects. He believes Anuun might be a key to 'awakening a greater conduit.' And he asked three different museum curators if they'd 'secured any skulls of immaculate lineage.'"

Laurie frowned. "'Immaculate lineage?' Sounds vaguely like eugenics."

"I agree," Dana whispered.

The third file read **Adrian Vale — Wealthy collector of magical objects**

"He's in his early sixties and aging like a well-kept secret, as somebody said on social media. Here's a good photo." Vale had silver hair that fell in neat, deliberate waves and eyes the color of antiqued gold. He was dressed in what looked like a bespoke charcoal suit with a pocket square matching his shirt.

"He's hosting a private solstice gala at his mansion tomorrow night."

"Why not on Solstice night?" Skye asked.

Maxwell just shrugged. "Security out the wazoo. Would be worth infiltrating if we can."

"But we're going to Celeste's workshop."

"Best to split up. I'll find a way to get in there. One of you will need to come," he said.

"Good plans," Jade said from the doorway.

Maxwell put his hand over his heart and gave her a nod.

Hoa burst in, cheeks rosy. "Are you done yet? The tree isn't going to decorate itself!"

John grinned. "Come on—let's help."

The kids dragged him away while Skye relit the candle that had sputtered. "Be ready for the ritual tonight," she said. "We're going to need every thread of magic we've got."

CHAPTER
TEN

Dusk sank over Red Fox Farm like a soft woolen mantle, dimming the orchard and whitening the pastures with frost. Torches flared to life around the stone circle, flames bowing to the winter wind. Above, the sky stretched deep and dark —a perfect canvas for the longest night.

Skye stepped into the circle's center, her green-and-gold cloak stirring around her ankles. Sprigs of oak and holly wove through her braid—symbols of the eternal dance of light and dark, the passing of the Holly King's rule, the rise of the Oak King's returning strength.

She raised her birch staff, carved with shining Celtic knotwork, and the gathered clan fell silent.

"Tonight," she said, her voice resonant and warm, "we honor Alban Arthan—the Light of Winter—the rebirth of the sun from the cradle of the longest night. Tonight we stand where our ancestors once stood, keeping vigil, waiting for the promise of dawn."

Skye circled the central firepit, dropping crushed rosemary, juniper, and cedar into the flames. Sparks leapt upward, swirling in golden spirals.

"These herbs were burnt in the old lands for cleansing and

protection," she continued. "Evergreens were kept in the home to remind all that life endures even in the coldest dark."

Everyone lifted the sprigs of cedar and pine they'd been given, the scents mingling with woodsmoke.

Skye raised her staff and touched flame to the first candle. One by one, the fire passed around the circle in a sunwise motion.

"From spark to spark," she said softly, "we kindle the newborn sun."

Candles lifted and glowed. Rosa sat tall beside Laurie, haloed by flickering light. Oliver stood sentinel-like, head high, warmed by the glow. Ashe and Taran patrolled just outside the circle. Cats came and went as they pleased, their magic not disturbing the sacred space.

When the last flame was lit, Skye stepped forward and extended her free hand toward the circle. "Before we cast our spells tonight," she said, "we call upon the sacred powers our foremothers called upon in their darkest hour."

She lifted her face to the torch-lit sky.

Brigid,
    Daughter of the Dawn,
    Keeper of the Eternal Flame,
    Goddess of Hearth and Healing,
    Poet of Inspiration—
    walk with us on this Solstice night.

A warm breeze stirred—impossible on such a cold evening—and several candles flickered but did not go out.

Skye continued, her voice soft but strong:

Brigid of the triple flame:
    Light our minds with clarity,
    Light our hearts with courage,
    Light our path with wisdom.
    Stand beside us

as the sun-child is reborn.
Bless this circle.
Bless this land.
Bless all who seek protection and truth this night.

The flames around the circle seemed to lift higher, as though answering.

Skye lowered her staff slightly and nodded to the group. "Speak now the blessing our ancestors spoke on winter nights—words carried through centuries."

Everyone raised their candles and recited together, voices weaving like threads of gold in the darkness:

Deep peace of the winter night to us.
　　Deep peace of the shining stars to us.
　　Deep peace of the hearth's warm light to us.
　　Deep peace of the returning sun to us.
　　May we walk protected.
　　May we walk in wisdom.
　　May we walk in light.

The words floated upward, settling into the night like sparks from the fire.

Silence followed—warm, reverent, expectant.

Skye pressed her hand to her heart. "By oak and flame, by Brigid's blessing, by the turning of the wheel—the light returns. And with it, the strength we need."

The fire surged, lifting embers into the dark.

The Solstice had fully begun.

Skye motioned for Laurie, Dana, and Maxwell to step forward. "We seek the truth of a relic lost," she said. "Not to take, but to safeguard. Not to claim dominion, but to prevent its misuse."

She motioned to a bowl of water, moonlit and still. "Place your hands above it. When we speak the words, hold Anuun in your mind —not its power, but its purpose."

Dana breathed steady and whispered, "Anuun, come into clarity."

Laurie added, "Reveal the path where you have gone."

Maxwell, a little awkward but earnest, said, "Show us who holds you and why."

Skye pressed her palm to the water. A faint glow rippled across its surface—white, then violet, then ember-bright.

Through earth, through flame,
    through shadow, through sky,
    Let the truth be seen.

The bowl shimmered—then a flicker of images rose like reflections. First a gloved hand, pale, ringed, distinctly aristocratic. Then the sound of water lapping. A velvet-lined case snapped shut. A shadow crossed the frame—tall, angular, wearing a dark coat.

Then the water stilled.

Skye exhaled. "Fairfax," she murmured. "But not alone."

Dana nodded. "Vale's presence was all over that vision."

Skye raised her arms to her sides and looked up at the stars. In her formal voice, she said, "Lead us to our ancient ancestor who is in peril. Help us save Anuun." She nodded at those who'd gathered around the bowl of water. Knowing this part of the ritual was finished, they moved back to their places in the circle.

Skye gathered three bundles of herbs—juniper, cedar, and sweetgrass—and tied them together with red thread.

"All who are here, step closer."

The circle tightened. Even the dogs edged in, who fortunately smell only of cedar and damp earth.

"May this place stand in safety," Skye said, raising the bundle. "May this family—by blood, by choice, by magic—stand shielded from deception, from ill intent, from harm."

She scattered salt in a wide arc. The torches snapped in sudden brightness.

The group repeated, "We are shielded. We are grounded. We are held."

Skye touched each person on the forehead with the herb bundle.

"By air's clarity."

On their chest. "By fire's courage."

On their shoulders. "By earth's strength."

On their hands. "By water's flow."

A warm pulse hummed through the clearing, like the land itself had breathed out a promise.

Skye lifted her face to the stars. "The night turns. The light returns. The path reveals itself."

Everyone echoed softly, reverently.

The fire crackled. A shooting star streaked across the sky, brief and brilliant.

Rosa whispered into Laurie's mind, *We're going to find that skull.* Oliver punctuated the promise with a solemn, approving woof.

The Yarrow clan broke into smiles, hugs, and laughter as the fire shifted from ritual flame to communal warmth.

The work would continue in the morning—tracking, confronting, outsmarting—but for tonight, under Solstice protection, they stood united.

"Time to feast," Fíona announced and everyone trooped into the house.

The kitchen was a riot of smells—rosemary and thyme, baked apples, melted butter—and Skye's parents, Fíona and Cormac, moved like a pair of merry sprites behind the counter. The Solstice buffet stretched across the farmhouse table, a feast of golds, greens, and reds that glowed in the candlelight.

"You guys should open a restaurant," Laurie said.

Cormac chuckled. "Been there, done that. Retired chef here, but I just can't stop cooking."

"Help yourselves before it gets cold," Fíona said, waving a wooden spoon like a wand.

John didn't need to be told twice. He reached for a slice of salmon en croûte, steam curling from the flaky crust, then added a heap of root-vegetable gratin glistening with cream. Laurie followed, balancing a bowl of pumpkin and chestnut bisque in one hand and snagging a forager's hand pie with the other. Dana, forgoing her usual glass of white wine, poured herself a mug of hot buttered rum, the aroma of cinnamon and clove chasing away the damp chill of the hovering conspiracy.

Minh, ever the bottomless teen, built a mountain of roasted greens, a chicken thigh, and oatcakes, while Maxwell cradled a mug of mulled cider and piled a plate high with salmon, vegetables, and cheese biscuits.

A few barks sounded and Grandfather Seamus walked out with four dog bowls piled high with what looked like fresh meat mixed with vegetables. Great, Laurie thought. Rosa was going to expect gourmet meals from now on.

Laurie felt the warmth of the food and the sounds of Skye's clan anchor her She looked around the table at her friends, the flicker of candle lights reflecting in their eyes.

A collective 'ooh' sounded from the living room. Hoa voice reached them, "It's so beautiful." They must have lit the tree.

Everyone drifted into the big room, drawn as if by gentle enchantment toward the towering Douglas fir. Ornaments shimmered among its branches, and tiny lights winked like constellations scattered through the needles. Laurie nodded as she set down her mug. The world outside might be cracking open with scandal and shadow, but something warm flickered inside her—a fragile, rising hope, bright and steady as the promise of the sun's return.

CHAPTER
ELEVEN

Skye wandered through Star, Stone & Flower, straightening shelves, checking stock, and readying the register drawers for the day. Someone had put on whale song—the low, haunting tones rolled through the shop like mist, punctuated by flute-like calls that rose and fell, echoing the pulse of the sea.

Then a faint sound broke through the music.

A kitten crying.

Skye cocked her head. The sound came from the back room. She frowned—something felt off, though she couldn't name what. Pushing open the door, she stopped short. The space was a chaos of paper and boxes. She'd just cleaned it yesterday. How had it exploded overnight?

She moved into the mess, shifting cardboard, scattering packing slips, searching for the tiny voice. The whale song deepened, urgent now, vibrating through the walls. Skye's stomach tightened. Something was wrong.

The kitten's cry shifted—stretching, unraveling—until it became a long, low sigh, almost human.

Skye...help me.

Her pulse leapt.

"Where are you?" she called aloud.

The world lurched.

Suddenly she wasn't in the shop anymore.

She stood barefoot in a vast rectangular chamber, its air dense with the scent of stone, smoke, and time. The floor beneath her feet was smooth wood, polished by centuries of ritual. Darkness pressed close around her—until a faint glimmer at the far end began to brighten, like the first breath of dawn.

Shapes emerged from the shadows.

Statues. Giants. Guardians.

Closest to her loomed Coatlicue, the serpent-skirted Mother. Although Skye wasn't familiar with this goddess, her name sprang into her mind. Two fanged faces merged at her neck in a fearsome double visage. Clawed hands gripped the edges of her writhing snake skirt. Power radiated from her—earth-deep and ancient enough to rattle Skye's bones.

To her right stood a life-sized Eagle Warrior, wings unfurled, feathers so finely carved they seemed to tremble. His stone eyes watched a horizon no human gaze could find.

Across from them, a figure of green-veined stone caught the rising glow: Medusa. Her serpentine hair writhed mid-motion, each snake frozen in a hiss. Yet there was sorrow in her face—a weariness born not of monstrosity, but of centuries of being feared. Her obsidian eyes glinted with warning. Skye felt a subtle, protective energy whisper around her ankles.

Next to her stood Kali, carved in obsidian-dark stone. Multiple arms fanned behind her like the petals of a deadly lotus. One hand held a curved blade; another offered a blessing. Her presence was fierce—but strangely comforting, like truth cutting through illusion.

Toward the end of the line waited Hades, carved from shadow-dark basalt. Cloaked in shifting stone, he held a helm that flickered between visibility and void. His deep-set eyes held neither welcome nor threat—only inevitability. Skye smelled pomegranate and cold stone, and the air tightened with the weight of thresholds.

And finally—at the far end, bathed in the chamber's growing light—sat Xōchipilli, the Flower Prince. His serene smile softened the room's edges. Blossoms, vines, and sacred mushrooms curled across his stone skin. Unlike the others, he radiated warmth—beauty, song, the breath after darkness. Skye felt her racing pulse calm just a fraction.

The light around him brightened until its source came into focus. Anuun.

At the end of the room was a raised platform. The crystal skull rested on an altar atop it, glowing like moonlight trapped in quartz.

Take me before it's too late.

Skye stepped forward, breath caught, hand reaching—

A touch on her shoulder.

"Skye, wake up."

Jade's voice pulled her back like a tide. She opened her eyes to the soft silver of moonlight falling across the dresser, the armchair, the rumpled quilt. Gandalf, curled on the blanket, lifted his head and meeped reassurance.

"Stars above," Skye whispered. "I was dreaming."

Jade sat up, reaching for the lamp.

"Leave it off." Skye turned to look at her wife, the moon outlining her cheek. "He called to me. I was in the store...then in a temple with statues—Coatlicue, Medusa, Kali, Hades...and the Flower Prince. I seemed to know all about them in the dream. And Anuun was on an altar, glowing."

"The magic is working," Jade said, her voice too excited for this early.

"Yes, it is," Skye whispered.

"Did you sense where it was?" Jade asked more gently this time.

Skye closed her eyes and sent out psychic feelers. The dream still hummed in her bones, the echo of whale song, the silent stone gods watching.

After a moment she opened her eyes. "Somewhere near. Seattle or close by. He said, *Take me before it's too late.*"

"Maybe Anuun will lead us to him."

"I hope so," Skye murmured. "What time is it?"

"Half past four. Try to sleep a little more."

"I can't. I'm going outside. Just be with the land."

Jade started to rise, but Skye laid a hand on her arm. "Stay. The dogs will keep me company. Maybe I'll hear him again."

"The thieves could be watching."

Skye smiled faintly. "Then Taran will eat them for breakfast."

Jade settled back with a sigh. "Shout if you need me."

"You'll feel it if something happens," Skye said, squeezing her hand. "We're tuned to each other."

She rose, padded to the living room, and shrugged into her coat.

Outside, the night was cool and wet, the garden silvered under a waning moon. The cedars whispered. The soil beneath her boots breathed, vital, alive. Somewhere distant, a coyote called. Skye lifted her face to the sky and let the world's quiet magic settle through her.

"Show me the way," she murmured to the unseen skull.

A faint hum answered in her bones.

If we keep walking past this school, they're going to get suspicious, Rosa said, her silky ears flicking in the chill breeze.

Oliver stopped dead in the middle of the sidewalk and gave a long-suffering sigh. *I'm tired. Let's go to the park instead.*

She tightened her grip on both leashes. "Our mark should be out any minute," she muttered, hoping to sound more confident than she felt.

Mark? Rosa said, tail swishing. *Been watching detective shows again?*

Laurie ignored the jab. She had a mission—ambush Jane Smith, a.k.a. Ravenna Crowhurst, right here at Laurelhurst Elementary. It seemed only fair. Ravenna had cornered Skye at *her* workplace first, playing mysterious High Priestess with questions about the skull. Turnabout was fair play.

The air smelled of wet cedar and petrichor. The school's brick facade glistened with rainwater, its windows glowing against the darkening afternoon. Maxwell had verified there was no faculty meeting or club Ravenna supervised after school today. Laurie could practically hear him now: *"Target leaves between 4:00 and 4:10, drives a blue Subaru, older model. Shouldn't be hard to spot."*

She still couldn't bring herself to call the woman Jane. Once you'd watched the tape of someone strutting into your friend's shop in a full Gothic ball gown and asking if the shop had a "crystal bust," it was hard to see her as *plain Jane.*

Laurie adjusted her scarf and settled on a bench closest to the parking lot. None of her former colleagues at Anthony University had ever heard of Dr. Victor Salazar. Rebecca, her friend from the English Department, said she knew some archaeologists at Harvard and would ask around, but Laurie didn't think she'd turn up anything.

The swings from the playground creaked in the wind, the sky a patchwork of gray and silver. Oliver sprawled out beside her with a contented grunt, his head resting on her boot. Rosa sat upright and watchful, ears pricked. The quiet hum of anticipation vibrated in Laurie's chest.

It wasn't just curiosity driving her—it was something deeper. Ever since the skull appeared, she'd felt...off. Restless. Like the world's edges were vibrating slightly out of sync. Confronting this "Ravenna Crowhurst" was the start to snapping things back into focus.

Maxwell had done a deep dive on her. Turns out she had a masters in English from the University of Washington. Did her thesis on Dickens, which explained her Victorian vocabulary. Except that outfit seemed more fitting for Stoker. She'd looked like something out of *Dracula.*

The door finally opened, releasing a few teachers who hurried toward their cars. Laurie's gaze sharpened. Not her. Another few minutes passed. Then the side door swung open again, and Ravenna emerged—no velvet cloak or glinting rings this time. Just a khaki pantsuit, dark red blouse, and a harried look that screamed overworked educator. Her blond hair was tucked under a knit beanie, and her briefcase bulged with papers.

Third graders didn't write essays, did they? What is she grading? Laurie wondered, remembering her professor days, trudging home burdened with papers. Twenty-five-page ones.

She stood and nudged Oliver's shoulder. "Come on, boy." He heaved a put-upon sigh but rose. She wanted Ravenna to see the boxer first. People usually took one look and gave her a wide berth, but Rosa trotted ahead like an emissary of chaos, tail high, eyes bright. Laurie crossed the parking lot, calling out cheerfully, "Ms. Smith? Jane Smith?"

Ravenna stopped. Her eyes flicked over Laurie, then the dogs. She tensed when she saw Oliver. "May I help you?"

"I wanted to ask a few questions—"

"Please make an appointment. It's really not appropriate to discuss students in parking lots." Her smile was brittle, forced.

"Oh, it's not about students." Laurie paused just long enough to savor the confusion. "It's about your visit to Star, Stone & Flower. And your threats against the owner."

Ravenna stiffened. "I—what? That's absurd—"

Rosa stepped forward, nose twitching. The teacher backed up. Laurie's irritation flared. How dare she flinch from Rosa. Her sweet, diplomatic little Havanese wouldn't hurt a fly—unless the fly insulted Skye, maybe.

A low growl rumbled in Oliver's throat.

Good boy, she sent to him.

"Please control your animals," Ravenna said tightly.

Laurie gave her a bright smile. "They look perfectly under control to me, *Ravenna Crowhurst.*"

The teacher's color drained. She went so pale she looked carved from wax. "You—you must have me confused with someone else. My name is—"

"Yes, Jane Smith, whose magical name is Ravenna Crowhurst."

A wash of red climbed her throat. "How did you find that out?"

"We have our ways," Laurie said. "What I want to know is why you were asking about the crystal—excuse me, what did you call it? The *crystal bust?*"

Ravenna's mouth twitched. "I don't know what you mean."

"We've got video," Laurie said. "Security cameras in the shop. We heard everything."

"We?"

Laurie smiled faintly. "The investigative team."

Oliver sat with a grunt. *I'm bored. Can we go home?*

Not yet, Laurie told him silently. *Play scary dog a bit longer.*

He huffed but stood, looming beside her.

"Who told you about the skull?" Laurie asked, voice soft but edged.

For a heartbeat, something flickered in Ravenna's eyes—greed, fascination, fear. "So, it's true," she breathed. "She has an ancient Atlantean skull."

"Had," Laurie said.

Ravenna's lips parted. "What do you mean?"

"It's been stolen. The police are involved."

Her hand flew to her chest. "Stolen?"

Laurie let silence hang between them like a net. "You don't strike me as the type who could pull off a heist like that."

Had it been a heist exactly? Laurie wondered, but she liked the sound of it.

"So, help me out, and I'll make sure the authorities don't bother asking awkward questions here at your place of employment." Laurie couldn't really stop them—they had the security footage— but might not make all the connections Maxwell had.

Ravenna glanced back toward the school doors, her nerves as obvious as the pulse beating at her throat.

"Who told you?" Laurie pressed.

A long moment passed before Ravenna whispered, "Someone from my...group."

"You mean your coven?"

Her eyes darted around. "That lady who runs the crystal skull healing sessions—she told him. They're...close."

"Celeste Ardolf?" Laurie asked.

Ravenna nodded quickly. "Yes, that's her."

"And the *him* in question?"

"I don't want to—"

Laurie straightened. "Fine. Then I'll have the police question everyone in the Eclipsed Circle of the Sacred Thirteen. I'm sure they'll love that."

Ravenna's shoulders sagged. "All right. His name is..." She hesitated, then whispered, "Dr. Lucien Harrow. He's the one who said the skull was real—Atlantean, powerful. He asked me to go to the shop and verify it."

Laurie tapped the name into her phone. "Why didn't he go himself?"

Ravenna's expression twisted with discomfort. "I was curious, all right? But I didn't steal anything. I swear it."

Laurie gave a slow nod. "Thank you for your cooperation."

"You didn't give me much choice."

"Don't leave town." Laurie pivoted sharply and started toward her car, the dogs falling into step beside her—Rosa trotting, Oliver trudging.

Why did you tell her not to leave town? Rosa asked.

Laurie smiled down at her. *Because I've always wanted to say that.*

TWELVE

Celeste Ardolf stood at the front of the room, her silver hair catching the lamplight like spun glass. The air in Celestial Crystal and Gems' back room shimmered faintly with frankincense and expectation. A red pillar candle surrounded by holly burned on the table and a small quartz skull beside it wore a miniature Santa hat. About a dozen people sat in a semicircle of mismatched chairs, notebooks open, eyes bright.

Skye sat with Laurie and Dana in the second row off to the side, hoping they were out of Celeste's view. In an undertone, she told them about her dream—seeing Anuun in the strange room with the row of statues. For some reason, she could still remember the names of the deities and she listed them off.

"You think that's where the thief took him?" Dana whispered.

Skye shrugged.

"Those gods and goddesses—they're all pretty dark," Laurie said, pulling out her English professor training. "Except for the Eagle Warrior and the Flower Prince. Not evil per se, although they might be mistaken for that. Not fun-loving, though. More like face-your-fear types."

"That's your take," Skye said, "but I had a feeling this temple was dedicated to the dark."

Laurie shrugged. "That magician might find himself disappointed."

Celeste cleared her throat and quiet settled like snow in the forest. Their host smiled. "Good evening, everyone. Thank you for joining me here tonight. We're stepping into one of my favorite mysteries—the realm of the crystal skull." She paused, letting the words hang for a moment. "These strange, luminous objects have stirred curiosity for more than a century, bridging the space between myth and material."

She turned slightly, gesturing to a beautiful rose quartz skull resting on the table beside her. A bit larger than Anuun, it glowed from the candles behind it. "Let's begin with what we know, or at least what historians think they know. Most of the skulls we hear about today—those in museums or private collections—are said to come from Central America. The British Museum and the Smithsonian each have one, and for years, they were presented as Aztec or Maya artifacts. But when scientists looked closer, they found traces of modern abrasives, tool marks from rotary wheels—technology that didn't exist in pre-Columbian times."

A murmur ran through the room. Celeste's eyes twinkled. "Does that mean they're fakes? Perhaps. But remember, authenticity isn't only about the date of creation. A crystal skull carved in the nineteenth century can still hold energy if it's charged with human intention. And crystal in and of itself is powerful. Objects absorb story, emotion, belief. They're like mirrors for consciousness."

Skye considered this idea. It resonated with her family's view that everything was created from consciousness and was therefore aware in some way. The modern concept that some things lived and others were just inanimate objects was not something she agreed with. Even her computer had a mind of its own at times, much to her consternation.

Celeste stepped closer to the group, lowering her voice. "Now, let's wander into legend. Some say there are thirteen ancient skulls scattered across the world. When they're reunited, humanity will experience a leap in awareness—a new dawn of understanding." Her smile turned hopeful.

Laurie leaned over and whispered. "Marco said something similar."

Skye nodded.

"Others claim they came from Atlantis or were shaped by beings from the stars. Whether you take that literally or not, myth always points to something deeper. Thirteen—symbol of transformation. The skull—symbol of memory and mortality. Quartz—the perfect conductor."

She picked up a smaller quartz skull and turned it in her hands. Light fractured through it in a thousand sparks. "Why quartz? Because quartz stores energy. This isn't just mystical talk—there's science in it. Quartz is piezoelectric. That means when it's squeezed or heated, it produces an electrical charge. That's why it's used in watches, radios, even computers. Its crystalline lattice is stable, but not solid. There are tiny spaces—microscopic gaps in the matrix—where energy can resonate, align, and, some say, *linger*."

Celeste tapped the skull lightly with one fingertip. "Imagine those gaps as little chambers of memory. When you hold a quartz crystal—or a skull carved from it—your energy field interacts with that lattice. Thought, emotion, intention—they all vibrate. The crystal receives that pattern and amplifies it. The skull form adds another layer—it mirrors the human mind, the seat of memory and spirit. So, what we have here is both symbol and amplifier. Consciousness looking back at itself."

The audience sat motionless, listening. Even Oliver had sat up, his eyes glinting.

"Of course," she went on, "science doesn't confirm any of this beyond the physical properties of quartz. But myth and meaning aren't confined to microscopes. The important thing is relationship. If you treat the skull as mere décor, it remains silent. If you approach it with respect and clear intention, it becomes a partner—a keeper of your thoughts, a teacher, sometimes even a trickster."

A hand rose from the second row. "So...are you saying they're alive?"

Celeste tilted her head thoughtfully. "Alive? Not the way we are. But they respond. They remember. Think of them as ancient libraries —repositories of vibration. They store what we feed them. Which means," she added, voice softening, "we must be mindful of what we give."

Skye was beginning to revise her opinion of this woman. Her empathic sense told her Celeste believed everything she was saying. Earnestly. And Skye agreed with her. Well, mostly. Anuun certainly seemed alive to her. A fully developed consciousness with a distinct personality. A crystal being. One who didn't need to be fed or have a litter box, like Thistle and Wild Rose. Thank the Goddess.

A soft chuckle sounded in Skye's mind. Amazed, she looked around for its source.

We are alive.

Skye tried to contain her surprise. The large rose skull was talking to her.

My keeper is coming along. The skull's tone was fond, as if speaking of a pet.

Uh, that's good, Skye said. *Thanks for connecting with me.*

Skye felt the rose skull's attention switch back to Celeste as the lecturer placed the smaller crystal back on the table. "When you work with a skull, clear it often. Moonlight, smoke, intention— whatever method suits your practice. Then, when you're ready, focus your thoughts. Let your heart align with the pattern of the quartz. Speak your purpose aloud or in silence. That vibration settles into the matrix. From then on, the skull carries it—until you change it or cleanse it again."

Celeste stepped back, folding her hands. "That's the secret of these so-called mysteries. Whether carved by an Aztec artisan or a Parisian jeweler, whether born of myth or marketing, the crystal skull is a vessel. It reflects what we put inside it—and perhaps, if we're lucky, what the universe wants us to remember."

She smiled, the room glowing with quiet awe. Even Skye was impressed, although she thought Anuun held more than what humans had put in him.

"She's not exactly what I expected," Laurie whispered.

"I was thinking the same thing," Skye answered in a low tone.

"Now," Celeste said, "let's experience a crystal skull for ourselves."

She turned to the rose quartz skull on the altar behind her. The candlelight caught the blush within the stone, casting warm reflections on the ceiling. "This," she said softly, "is Seraphina. Her name came to me in meditation—unbidden, as such things do."

She lifted the skull with both hands and carried it to the center of the circle. "She's carved from Madagascar rose quartz. If clear quartz is about clarity and focus, rose quartz is the keeper of compassion, forgiveness, and love. When those qualities fuse with the skull form, you get a consciousness that helps to heal."

The group leaned forward, breath held.

"Now," Celeste said, voice barely above a whisper, "remember what I told you about resonance? The lattice responds to energy. This skull has sat with ancient ones and attuned to their vibration, taking on their knowledge. So, let's listen."

She placed Seraphina gently on a low oak stool draped in linen. Celeste lit a few tea lights around it. The stone caught a flicker of flame and seemed, for an instant, to glow from within.

Skye felt it first—a low vibration in her chest, like a tuning fork struck in her heart rather than her ears. The air thickened, sweet with the scent of roses.

Celeste's eyes widened slightly, though her calm never faltered. "Ah," she murmured, "she's responding."

The rose-quartz skull shimmered again, a faint pulse rising and fading like a heartbeat. "Everyone take three deep breaths and release them fully. Look at Seraphina but let your focus be soft."

Celeste inclined her head toward the crystal. "She carries memory," she said. "Sometimes it's personal, sometimes collective. Sometimes..." Her gaze met Skye's, knowing, "it's ancient."

Skye swallowed hard. The pulse in her chest quickened, matching the rhythm of the light. A whisper brushed her thoughts—soft, melodic, like breath through glass.

One of starlight, the skull said, *you remember the songs, don't you?*

A silver tear traced a path down Skye's cheek. Yes, she did remember the songs. Star songs. Sometimes she could hear them singing.

I'll help you find the Pure One, Seraphina said.

This time Skye jerked back in her chair, unable to contain her shock.

"Skye?" Laurie's voice came gently. "You okay?"

Skye forced a smile, though her pulse still fluttered. "Yeah," she whispered. "She just...said hello."

Maybe Celeste wasn't involved with the theft after all, Skye thought. Perhaps she'd felt Anuun arrive somehow. Skye could feel the woman had some psychic ability. Maybe her skull had told her. She felt a surge of affirmation from the gorgeous rose quartz.

The group sat in awed silence as the glow dimmed to a gentle blush, like the last trace of sunset through rose glass. Celeste bowed her head in respect, then gently called the group back. "Be aware of your body in the chair, your breath. Feel your feet on the floor. It's time to return, but we come back with the gift she's given us."

A few people in the group sniffled, reaching into their pockets or purses for tissues. Others sat in quiet reverence.

"She speaks in vibration," she said. "Not all will hear her the same way. Sometimes it's a whisper, sometimes an image, sometimes just a warmth in the heart. Sometimes her message comes later, in dreams or quiet moments. But remember—she's not simply a tool. She's a teacher. And tonight, she's awake."

Outside, the wind rattled the chimes hanging in the shop's doorway. The sound was faint but unmistakably musical, as if the whole building were listening too.

Celeste had several mid-size skulls sitting around Seraphina, rose, clear and smokey quartz, an amethyst. Beside them was a basket of small ones. "These skulls are available to buy if anyone is so inclined. They hold Seraphina's energy. They make lovely gifts to the right person or you might want one for yourself. I'm available for personal readings also."

People crowded around, picking up the crystals, talking with each other. Celeste took their purchases on her iPad. Skye and Laurie waited, wanting to talk to her in private. When the last of the clients left and the scent of frankincense and candle smoke had faded to a faint sweetness, only five remained: Celeste, Skye, Laurie with Rosa curled up like a small cloud of fur at Laurie's feet. Oliver sat beside them, solemn as a wise one.

Celeste set Seraphina back on the altar, her expression thoughtful. "It's been a long time since she stirred that strongly," she said. "I'd forgotten how the air feels afterward. Like the room's remembering itself."

Skye nodded, though she couldn't quite meet her gaze. Her fingers still tingled from the vibration that had run up her arm when Seraphina pulsed. "She's extraordinary," Skye murmured, then chose her words carefully, not revealing her true thoughts. "She's almost alive."

"Well," Celeste said with a small, knowing smile, "alive enough." She passed her hand slowly over the candle flame as if gathering stray energy. "Rumor has it that you might be in possession of an ancient skull yourself, Skye. Is that true?"

The question came lightly, but Skye felt its weight. She hesitated, brushing her palms against her jeans. "I—where did you hear that?"

"Word travels fast in our little circles." Celeste's tone was airy, but her eyes remained sharp. "A friend mentioned something about unusual activity in your shop. I thought perhaps you'd received a visit from one of the elders."

Skye glanced at Laurie, who lifted an eyebrow but said nothing. "Maybe," Skye said slowly. "Depends what you mean by *visit*."

Celeste's smile deepened. "Oh, I think you know what I mean."

Skye tilted her head. "Do you know Ravenna Crowhurst?" she asked, careful to keep her voice even.

A shadow passed over Celeste's face—something that might have been amusement or regret. "I wouldn't call her an elder. She's a bit—how can I put this—*dramatic*. Rather new to the craft."

She reached for a small amethyst point next to Seraphina and turned it over in her hand. "I heard she turned up at your shop, asking about a 'crystal bust.'"

Skye chuckled. "Yes, dressed for a Samhain party."

Celeste gave a small, rueful smile. "It might have been my fault, actually. I spoke to Lucien about what Seraphina seemed to be picking up. Her impressions are—how shall I say—broad strokes. Feelings more than facts. There was something about an energy disturbance, a missing artifact, maybe another skull. I thought Lucien should know."

Skye's pulse quickened. "And you told Ravenna?"

Celeste's fingers tightened around the stone. "No. At least, not directly. But Lucien...he has his ways of spreading information. I didn't realize she was involved until I heard she paid you a visit."

Celeste's shop fell quiet. The only sound was the faint creak of the building and Rosa's slow breathing.

In the back of Skye's mind, a whisper stirred—soft, cool, and unmistakably feminine. *Please...protect Anuun.*

The words slid through her like smoke, leaving her skin prickling. Skye blinked and looked at Seraphina. The skull sat perfectly still on the altar, but the pink within it glowed faintly, like embers under ash.

Celeste followed her gaze. "Sometimes she hums after a reading," she said. "Residual energy. Nothing to worry about."

"Right," Skye said quietly, though she wasn't sure what Celeste had picked up. There was something guarded in Celeste's tone, a faint hesitation that didn't match her usual poise.

"You mentioned an elder?" Skye asked.

"Did anyone else come asking about the artifact?"

Skye felt the deception in her question. Celeste knew exactly who had come to the shop.

"Star, Stone & Flower gets quite crowded this time of year. If someone did, he—" she stumbled, realizing she might be giving away more than she wanted to "—or she might have spoken to one of my workers."

Celeste's eyes narrowed, but she gave Skye a quick smile.

Laurie glanced between them. "Well, this has been fascinating," she said lightly, reaching down to clip Rosa's leash. "But I think it's past someone's bedtime."

Rosa yawned, tail thumping once.

Celeste rose and smoothed her shawl. "Do take care, both of you," she said. "And if Seraphina's energy feels too strong, you know where to find me."

Skye tried not to react. Too strong? This woman had seriously underestimated her. Skye simply said, "Thanks, we will."

They stepped out into the cool evening. The shop door clicked shut behind them, muting the warm light inside.

Laurie waited until they'd reached the car before speaking. "Skye," she said quietly, "Rosa caught something in there."

Skye frowned. "What do you mean?"

Laurie bent to scratch the dog's head. "She recognized a scent. The same one she found after the skull went missing."

Skye stopped walking. "You're saying the thief—"

Laurie nodded. "Rosa smelled him in Celeste's shop."

For a moment, neither spoke. A wind stirred down the street, carrying the faint chime of shop bells and the lingering perfume of frankincense.

Skye looked back at the darkened window where Seraphina's soft glow still shimmered faintly behind the glass. "You know, that skull asked me to protect Anuun."

Laurie's eyes went wide. "Really?"

"And now we know the thief has been there," she said. "I hope he was just snooping around. Otherwise, we've got a bigger problem than I thought."

THIRTEEN

Adrian Vale knew how to stage an entrance—even to his own party.

His mansion perched on a forested bluff above Puget Sound, its sweeping windows drinking in the lights of passing boats. Tonight, the long drive glowed with lanterns shaped like bronze wyverns, their mouths exhaling flickering tongues of magic-blue flame. A string quartet played something lush beneath the porte cochère, though every now and then a discordant shimmer suggested a spell woven into the notes.

Maxwell took it all in with a silent whistle as he balanced a tray of smoked salmon bites. "Rich people really do live on a different planet," he murmured to Dana, who was buttoning the top of her waiter's vest and praying no ghosts decided to chat mid-service.

"Focus," she whispered back, tightening her ponytail. "We're here for intel, not hors d'oeuvres."

But the moment they stepped inside, the *wealth* hit them like a scented wave: cedar polished to mirror shine, beeswax candles floating in crystal globes, flowers enchanted to put people at ease and loosen lips. Guests mingled beneath a vaulted ceiling carved with celestial sigils—*old* ones, not the modern Seattle metaphysical boutique kind.

They had studied the guest list ahead of time. Now they picked out faces. Marsha Ferguson, who supposedly cheated at online gambling using proprietary tech.

Winton Foster of CyberCoast Technologies, laughing too loudly beside a French actress draped in silver silk. A state senator whose reputation for "green philanthropy" had been shredded earlier that week by anonymous leaks hinting at offshore accounts. A mystery school arch magus in a black tux—no, in the right light deep violet.

And in the middle of it all, hosting with a smile that never reached his eyes: Adrian Vale, tall, silver-streaked, elegant in a midnight-black suit that shimmered faintly with a glamour spell. He held a glass of something golden and probably magical.

Dana shivered. "He looks like someone who collects people the same way he collects artifacts."

"He does," Maxwell said under his breath.

The heart of the mansion was a sweeping, open expanse where guests drifted in glittering clusters, their murmured conversations rising and falling like a mesmerizing tide. Floor-to-ceiling windows framed the black-silver sheen of Puget Sound, the moonlight rippling across the water as if in answer to the music floating from the hidden quartet. Polished marble floors reflected the warm glow of suspended chandeliers—each one a branching constellation of glass shards twinkling like starlight. Dana thought there must be magic involved.

Sculptures and rare artifacts stood on discreet pedestals around the room, creating pockets of fascination where CEOs, senators, and sorcerers gathered to gossip. The air carried a blend of candle wax, winter roses, and faint ozone from magical wards thrumming beneath the party's polished surface. Waiters—Maxwell and Dana among them—glided through the crowd with silver trays, the guests accepting delicacies and champagne without ever looking at the servers' faces, already too engrossed in hushed conversations about power, influence, and secrets. The two spies listened for any hints of a stolen artifact.

Dana noticed Vale subtly moving certain people into an alcove where a row of glass cases displayed small figurines and stone slabs covered in hieroglyphs. She maneuvered her way closer so she could overhear their conversation. Vale joined them and said in a low voice, "If you'll join me, I thought I'd show you the newest additions to my collection."

There were appreciative murmurs. A few greedy smiles.

Maxwell and Dana, blending in with another caterer, followed the group down a hallway lined with ancient masks whose eyes seemed to follow them. A faint psychic pressure buzzed in Dana's temples—ghosts lingering maybe, not fully manifest. She fervently hoped she didn't have any ghostly encounters tonight.

Vale unlocked a bronze door with a key as old as any European empire. Inside, the temperature dropped to museum cold. Crystal cases filled the room like a private Louvre of dangerous magic: obsidian knives, runestones, and a length of braided gold. Vale waved his hand toward it. "A Tibetan Bonpo explained this rope was rumored to bind spirits."

The group moved to the next case holding—Dana's breath hitched—a carved stone skull the size of a grapefruit. Not Anuun, but from the same lineage. The hum of power around it was unmistakable.

A guest, a CEO with a sinister sneer, lifted his brows. "Something new, Adrian? It looks rather modern."

Vale smiled thinly. "I only collect real."

Dana shot Maxwell a look. He gave the slightest nod. *This* was where the answers lay.

Vale moved from item to item, giving brief histories. Often sanitized. Sometimes wrong, Dana thought. But he spoke with the easy pride of a man who knew no one here would dare contradict him.

"Here we have the Aureate Cipher." He pointed to a palm-sized golden disk covered in spiraling sigils. "These rearrange themselves depending on lunar phases.

It came from an early 1900s British occult order, rumored to have been smuggled out of an excavation in Egypt. It allows the user to decode ancient ritual texts otherwise locked behind magical encryption."

"And this is the Key of Severin." He pointed to a wrought-iron device with runic teeth. He opened the case and picked it up, then handed it to the mage beside him. "Warm to the touch despite its age. Part of a lost set of ritual keys used in 19th-century European spirit lodges."

The man handed it back. "Intriguing."

"It unlocks spirit thresholds, small metaphysical doors that allow powerful entities to slip into the mortal plane briefly. One key alone grants access to partial thresholds, enough for visions, ghosts, or psychic bleed-through."

A witch beside the arch magus whispered, "Fairfax helped him acquire that one," nodding toward a blue-green sphere swirling with internal mist.

Fairfax. Skye's mysterious aristocrat. Vale's elegant, unknowable cousin. Dana drifted closer, offering canapes.

The witch continued, "I told him meddling with those...artifacts...would come back to haunt him. But that family—always thinking they can horde what they take."

"Indeed?" the arch magus asked softly.

"Oh, you know." Her eyes glittered. "If they come around, be sure to lock up your valuables."

Dana pretended not to hear, but her pulse quickened. Apparently, the Fairfax-Vale line did not come by their relics honestly.

Another guest—a woman from an old family—laughed and said, "If Reginald Fairfax is mixed up in this latest scandal, maybe Adrian should rein him in. A family empire only stays powerful if its secrets stay quiet."

Dana froze, tray hovering mid-air. *Scandal. Secrets. Family empire.*

Maxwell caught the exchange from across the room and raised a brow: *Get more.*

She moved closer.

"Is Reginald coming tonight?" her companion asked.

The councilwoman wrinkled her nose. "Adrian said he was 'abroad on urgent business.' Which usually means hunting down some artifact no one should even know exists."

The man she was with chuckled.

Dana's heart thudded. Vale was lying. Reginald Fairfax was in Seattle.

"Let's rejoin the party," Vale said in a voice that cut through the murmur of conversation. "We wouldn't want our absence to be noticed."

The group followed him. The door opened into the smaller alcove adjoining the large open area. The magical people flowed into the more mundane guests without a ripple. Dana retreated to the kitchen to grab a full tray of canapes.

"Crap," Maxwell whispered in the hall.

"What?"

Maxwell shook his head at Dana. His watch sent a faint prickle on the back of his arm. An alarm that told him his equipment just got noticed.

In a side hallway lined with carved wooden saints and demons, one of his micro-cams flickered. He saw it through his wrist device: a clear feed, then static, then—

A hand lifted the camera.

Turned it toward a face.

A face Maxwell recognized.

Adrian Vale stared straight into the lens, expression calm. Too calm. Then he crushed the camera under the heel of his Dior calfskin oxfords.

Maxwell's blood went cold.

Two seconds later the alarm went off—not a screaming klaxon, nothing gauche—just a subtle but unmistakable ripple through the mansion's wards, a shimmer in the air that made half the magicians lift their heads like hounds catching scent and the mundane guests shift uncomfortably, looking around for something to explain their unease.

Vale's voice carried, smooth as poured mercury but edged with steel. "It seems someone has placed unauthorized devices in my home."

The atmosphere snapped tight.

Guests murmured—some offended, others intrigued. A tech mogul whispered, "Corporate espionage?"

Someone else hissed, "Political spying?"

A witch with an elaborate pentagram necklace muttered, "Foolish. Very foolish."

Vale's gaze swept the room like a blade. "I apologize for the interruption. Please remain where you are. My staff will conduct a brief sweep."

Dana felt Maxwell appear at her elbow like a conjured ghost. "We need to go," he murmured.

"No," Dana whispered, eyes narrowing. "We need to stay just long enough to see how he reacts—and what he reveals."

Vale lifted the crushed camera between two fingers. "Whoever did this will find themselves...enlightened. Thoroughly."

A ripple of nervous laughter moved through the room.

Then Vale smiled, too pleasant. "And if my cousin has been involved in anything untoward recently—well. I do hope it wasn't *this*." His tone dripped implication. "Reginald has always been... impulsive."

The guests buzzed.

Dana and Maxwell exchanged a look. Did Vale just throw Fairfax under the bus? Or was he planting a misdirection? Either way, the disruption had cracked the party's perfect veneer, exposing a layer of tension that felt ripe with answers. But also extremely dangerous.

Maxwell whispered, "We're in trouble."

"Probably," Dana murmured. "But at least we're getting somewhere."

And above them, unnoticed, one of Maxwell's *other* cameras—cleverly nestled in a glittering chandelier—continued recording.

The mansion's ambiance shifted the moment Vale dismissed the alarm. Conversations resumed, but the edges were sharper now, charged with suspicion and veiled accusation. Servers bustled nervously. Magicians reinforced subtle wardings with flicks of their fingers.

Dana nudged Maxwell. "I'm going back into the artifact room. I felt a presence there."

"You realize he's going to double the wards now?"

"Yes," she said, lifting her catering tray. "Which means he's rattled. If there is a ghost, maybe he or she will talk."

Maxwell sighed and drifted off in another direction, head down, blending with staff.

The artifact room was dimmer now, as if the lights themselves felt chastised. Guests had mostly filtered back into the main hall, leaving only the lingering hum of too many magical objects in one place.

Bracing herself, Dana stepped inside, closing the door behind her with her hip. A ripple of cold slid across her arms.

"Here we go," she whispered.

A figure shimmered near the far case— faint, translucent, like light refracting underwater. A man in early 20th-century attire: waistcoat, wire-rim glasses, and the anxious energy of someone who had died prematurely and still wasn't over it.

Dana lifted her tray instinctively, as if the ghost needed canapés.

The spirit looked around sharply, then at her. *You can see me?*

Dana nodded, careful not to speak out loud. Someone might be listening.

The ghost drifted closer, the air dropping another ten degrees. His lips didn't quite move when he spoke, but the words hit her mind clearly. *You should leave this place.*

Dana gulped. *Believe me, working on it.*

He's dangerous, you know. The ghost cast a jittery glance toward the door. *Our host. Vale. He didn't kill me, but he ruined me. Took what was mine. Made sure no one ever found out.*

Dana's pulse jumped. *Took what?*

The ghost indicated the object in the case he hovered next to: a sharp triangular shard of black glass carved with precise angles. *The Obsidian Gnomon, once part of a powerful ritual sundial. Originally from a temple in Mesoamerica, but it was stolen during an expedition.*

Dana frowned at the plain shard, wondering what power it had. It looked just like an ordinary piece of obsidian.

The ghost sensed her confusion. *It can bend or compress "magical time" around a ritual for a brief window.*

That means Vale can create an interface with any era he chooses?

Exactly. The ghost quivered with anger. *I catalogued and protected the artifact during a museum acquisition, but Vale stole it just before it was scheduled for a public display.*

The ghost flickered, form thinning. *Artifacts. Always artifacts. He covets them. Needs them for what's coming.*

She leaned forward. *What's coming?*

The ghost's voice dropped to a psychic whisper sharp enough to sting. *A ritual. Christmas Eve. I know he's gathered some of the most powerful magicians for it. That they'll use the Obsidian Gnomon. But for what? To go when? I can't say.*

Dana felt the echo of his fear vibrate through her spine.

Go, he urged. *Before he knows you're here.*

The lights flickered. Steps approached—two sets, heavy, deliberate.

Dana pivoted, snatching a cloth from her tray and pretending to clean the floor around the glass case. The ghost dissipated like mist.

The door opened.

Adrian Vale stepped inside. He was alone.

Except—no. A shadow detached itself from the wall behind him, one of Vale's private security men. Not magical, but armed, and trained to spot anything out of place.

"Just finishing up in here," Dana chirped, cheerful as a game show host. "One of your ghosts spilled something syrupy. I wanted to clean it before it hardened."

Vale smiled without warmth. "I appreciate diligence."

His gaze swept the room. Too slow. Too assessing.

"Have you seen anything unusual tonight?" Vale asked pleasantly.

Dana's heart skipped. "Just a lot of very hungry people."

Vale chuckled. "Indeed."

But as he stepped closer, that chuckle turned thoughtful.

"For some reason," he murmured, "I feel like something has shifted."

Dana shrugged, made her eyes round. "I'm sorry, sir. I don't..." She let her sentence trail off and held her breath.

He finally turned and left, the guard ghosting after him.

The real ghost did not reappear.

Meanwhile, Maxwell worked his way toward the service stairwell, the one he'd mapped earlier as a safe route to check on his remaining devices. He reached into the narrow alcove behind a statue of a horned Celtic deity, fingers brushing the tiny camera tucked in the baseboard—

A hand clamped onto his shoulder.

Maxwell's soul nearly left his body.

"YOU."

He turned slowly.

The head caterer glared at him, eyes blazing. "You're supposed to be on appetizers, not skulking around in restricted areas!"

"Oh—right! Sorry! I thought this was—uh—storage?"

"Storage?! That staircase leads to the family wing!"

Maxwell stared. "I'm new."

"I can tell."

As she stomped off, muttering about incompetent temp staff, Maxwell sagged against the wall.

Then he froze. Because from behind the statue, he heard two voices.

Whispers. Only fragments.

"...ritual must be completed on the twenty-fourth..."

"...Fairfax swears the artifact is secured..."

"...it must be the genuine one. The others won't open the gateway..."

Maxwell pressed himself flatter, heart pounding.

"...Vale thinks no one suspects him, but if people are searching for it—"

The voices cut off as footsteps approached. Maxwell darted away just in time, nearly dropping his tray of empty champagne flutes.

Dana found him by the back doors leading to the deck, where cool air from the Sound brushed in.

"You look like you saw a basilisk," she whispered.

"Close," he muttered. "Corporate caterer."

Dana huffed a quiet laugh. "I talked to a ghost."

"...You win."

Dana grabbed his sleeve. "The ghost said Vale's planning a ritual. On Christmas Eve."

Maxwell blanched. "I heard that too. And they mentioned an artifact—the real one. They need the real one to open something."

They stared at each other.

"Has to be Anuun," Dana said.

Maxwell nodded grimly. "We have to warn the others."

Behind them, the party continued—music, light, laughter.

But the Sound roared below the cliffside, dark and cold and restless, as though it knew something old and dangerous was stirring beneath the holiday cheer.

CHAPTER

FOURTEEN

T he next morning, Laurie sat on the couch in her parents' family room, a pouty cat on her lap demanding attention. And explanations. Laurie had come here first thing because last night had run so late, she hadn't visited Natasha. Truth be told, she'd celebrated with John and had one too many Frambozens, her favorite raspberry Christmas beer, to be safe to drive. Now she was paying the piper. The cat, that is.

Where are my humans? I've been alone here for years. Decades.

Natasha kneaded her lap more vigorously than Laurie thought was strictly necessary. She was glad she'd worn her denim with the flannel lining. Kept out the chill and the needle point cat claws.

"They've only been gone three days. They'll be home tomorrow." Laurie spoke aloud, knowing the sound of her voice helped to soothe the Russian Blue.

And where have you been taking Oliver? He's been having fun and I'm stuck here. Why can't I come?

"You don't like riding in cars and we've been in meetings with lots of people."

People? Like when you bring your friends over and John, too? That many?

"Way more. Sometimes thirty in one room."

Natasha dug in her claws and hissed.

Laurie winced. "Right? I knew you wouldn't like that. Plus, we're in strange rooms. Three different ones so far."

When will humans learn to stay in their own territory and not wander all over?

"We're very different from cats."

Oliver says somebody stole a talking rock. What's so special about that? Everything talks—trees, bushes, rocks, birds, even mice. Yum, I like mice.

Laurie chuckled. She stroked the cat, scratched under her chin and behind her ears, and told her all about Anuun. How he'd suddenly appeared, surprising Skye, then told her his name. How he lit up a room and made everyone feel peaceful.

Like me, then.

Laurie bit her lip to keep from laughing. "Yes, just like you. But he's much older. Some people say he was carved in Atlantis. Some say he came from the stars eons ago."

I was a temple cat at Karnak.

Laurie's hands stilled in surprise until Natasha nudged her with a paw.

You were there, too. And mom.

"You'll have to tell me about this life some time," Laurie said.

I could tell you now. We have a whole day and tonight. Where will the sun be when my humans return?

Laurie decided it was safest to answer the second question first. "When the sun is heading down toward the mountains, but before it goes behind them."

So, about 2:30.

"How'd you get so smart?" Laurie scratched down both sides of Natasha, adding just the pressure the cat loved.

I've always been this smart. Now I'll tell you about our days in Egypt.

"I need to tell you one more thing about Anuun."

Natasha let out a little grunt of dissatisfaction.

"He's been stolen."

Who took him?

"We don't know. But I promised to help Skye find out. Today is the day before Christmas Eve and her store will be extra busy—"

Too many people.

"Exactly, so I promised her I'd follow one of the suspects to see if he has Anuun hidden somewhere."

Natasha stopped purring.

"Do you want me to leave Oliver here for company?"

He'll sleep all day and he snores.

Natasha would sleep all day, too. Laurie quieted the thought before the cat picked up on it.

I am abandoned by all and will suffer my exile in silence.

Laurie didn't point out that to be exiled meant to be thrown out of your home. "I'm so sorry, sweet one. Shall I give you some of the extra sharp catnip and some whipped cream to celebrate the turn of the seasons?"

Natasha was silent for so long, Laurie wondered if she'd gone to sleep.

That would be small recompense to repay me for my suffering, but it is an acceptable beginning.

"Plus, I'll open a can of tuna for you."

Natasha jumped down and trotted into the kitchen where she sat by her bowl, eyeing Laurie's every move. Laurie put a dollop of whipped cream on a saucer and placed it before the cat. It wasn't enough cream to upset her digestion. Natasha licked it up and sat cleaning her face while Laurie upended a can of Albacore tuna (line caught, of course—her mother wouldn't have any other kind) into a bowl.

"Madam," she said as she placed the bowl before Natasha.

Oliver and Rosa started toward it. "No, you're coming with me.

This is for the cat." She escorted the boxer and little Havanese into the living room and closed the door.

Oliver whined.

Serves him right, Natasha said, licking the tuna juice up first.

Laurie rolled her eyes. Before she'd started hearing their thoughts, she would never have guessed the emotional lives of animals were so complex. Digging into the back of the pantry, she finally found the air-tight bag of special catnip harvested from her mom's summer garden. Laurie cut the bag open, and the pungent, peppery smell filled the air. She laid it all on a kitchen towel. It would be all over the floor tomorrow morning, but she'd sweep it up before her parents got home.

Natasha gave it a sniff. *This is acceptable. Perhaps I shall forgive you in our next life.*

Honestly, Laurie thought. She reached down to give Natasha one more scratch and was rewarded by a swipe. Felines always got feisty when nip was involved. To demonstrate, Natasha took a zoom around the family room, leaping onto the back of the sofa, then down and around. She ended back where she started.

Laurie grabbed her keys and headed to the living room. "Let's go, big boy. We've got a thief to catch."

John had fully charged the Leaf before heading off this morning to his first meeting with the planning committee for tidal energy development. The dogs jumped in the back and they headed toward downtown. Sometime last night or in the wee hours, Maxwell had planted a tracking device on Victor Salazar's phone—she had no clue how. Did he ever sleep?

At a red light, she clicked on the icon that showed her prey's location. Or his phone's. She sincerely hoped he was as attached to it as most people were and had it with him. A red dot appeared just up from the ferry docks in the Cascadia Grand, the hotel Salazar had checked into. So, he was still in his room or somewhere in the vicinity.

Then she realized she didn't know how he was getting around.

Was he taking the bus or had he rented a car. She sent a text to Maxwell, keeping one eye on the light.

> DANA: Did Salazar rent a car? 🚗
>
> MAXWELL: You woke me up for this?
>
> DANA: So you do sleep. 🛌
>
> MAXWELL: When people let me. And the emojis are supposed to substitute for the words.
>
> DANA: 🔫
>
> MAXWELL: 🐕 Checking.
>
> DANA: Thanks.

A car horn sounded from behind her. Laurie jerked her attention back to the road and took off, giving the driver behind her an apologetic wave. The car passed her and the driver put up his hand in a rude gesture. Oh well, Laurie thought, and headed down Marion. She chose to ignore the beep on her phone that told her Maxwell had answered her already. Somebody pulled out of a parking spot on the street a block up from the Cascadia Grand and she grabbed it, thanking the powers that be. Then she read the text.

> MAXWELL: Black Volvo, license QRI-3574
>
> DANA: Thank you. Now go back to 🛌

Laurie settled in to watch the hotel. Oliver snored. Rosa hopped into the front passenger seat and kept a sharp lookout.

What's he look like?

She found a picture of Salazar on the web and held it up to Rosa. The little dog pushed it away with her paw. *I can't really see that tiny box.*

Should I describe him to you?

Just look at the picture—every detail—and I'll see it in your mind.

This animal communication thing just kept getting better and better. Laurie studied the image of Dr. Victor Salazar. He looked like a man who'd spent decades in harsh landscapes and then never truly returned. In his late 50s, his graying hair curled at the temples, and a scruffy beard shadowed a face lined from sun, wind, and too many sleepless nights. His steel-gray eyes were sharp and haunted, calculating, as if he waited for something only he could see. His skin was deeply tanned, his hands calloused—still an explorer's hands, even if his work had taken a...darker turn. He dressed in expedition gear softened by age: cargo pants, beat-up boots, and a threadbare canvas coat that Laurie guessed smelled faintly of ash, earth, and incense used in rituals he shouldn't be performing. He held an Indiana Jones style fedora in his hand.

Got it, although I could have done without the poetry.

Geez, you been taking snark lessons from Natasha?

The little Havanese mix licked her cheek in apology. Then she moved into Laurie's lap and put her front paws on the doorframe. Laurie enjoyed the warmth and company.

An hour passed.

I'm bored, Rosa said.

Me, too.

After another half hour, Oliver woke up and stretched. He struggled to sit up in the small seat and was finally successful just as Laurie reached back to help him.

I need a bush, he announced.

Laurie looked around and saw a small strip of green next to the hotel. She got the dogs out of the car and on their leashes, and they made their way to the big leaf maple surrounded by rhododendrons and serviceberry bushes. She was glad to see the city was planting more flowering shrubs that fed the birds and bees. If only they could save the orcas.

Oliver plowed into the middle of a bush and squatted. She fished in her purse for a poop bag and just as she leaned over to pick up his droppings, Victor Salazar sauntered by.

Great, she thought. *He got a good glimpse of my behind.*

What's wrong with that? Oliver asked at the same time that Rosa said, *That's him. That's our quarry.* She started after him, leash trailing.

"Wait," Rosa hissed, trying not to draw the prey's attention, but it was too late. Salazar grabbed Rosa's leash and said, "Hello, little one. I think you left your human behind."

Rosa was busy sniffing him all over. Well, as far up as she could reach.

Laurie tied off the poop bag, dropped it in the nearby trash can, and walked out with Oliver in tow. Salazar stood in the middle of the sidewalk, holding Rosa's leash.

Rosa gave her a mournful look. *I've been captured.*

"Did you lose someone?" Salazar asked, holding out the little Havanese's leash.

Laurie froze for a split second. How could she follow someone who'd gotten a good look at her face? She took the leash slipping her hand into the leather loop. "Thank you so much. These streets are so busy." Laurie cringed. Could she sound more like a dingbat? "I didn't want her dashing into traffic."

Rosa sniffed. *I'm not a moron.*

I know.

"A boxer, too. Quite different dogs." Salazar gave her a little salute and turned to walk away.

"He's my parents' dog." She might as well take advantage of the situation. See what she could learn. "They're visiting Palenque. My father's an archaeologist."

Liar, Rosa said.

Play along.

They fell in step. "What a coincidence. That is my profession as well."

"Really? What's your specialty?"

"The Maya, classical period." Salazar jutted his chin forward.

Laurie plastered an awed look on her face. "How fascinating."

Salazar puffed up a bit. "I've studied many ancient sites in Central and South America. My primary interest is in artifacts—objects the indigenous shamans used in their ceremonies."

Laurie knew that no legitimate archaeologist would use the word 'shaman' since the word originated from the steppes of Siberia, but she didn't let this show. "Ooh, like magic?" she asked, nudging a bit more bimbo into her tone.

You're embarrassing us, Rosa said.

What's wrong with her? Oliver asked.

She's trying to fool the human. Males are gullible, Rosa said.

Oliver stopped walking. *You don't have to be rude.*

I mean human males.

Laurie felt a jolt as she came to the end of Oliver's leash. She looked back at the boxer standing stock still in the middle of the sidewalk. She slapped the side of her leg. "Come on, boy."

I am not gullible, Oliver said.

What? Laurie frowned. She'd only been vaguely aware of the conversation between the dogs.

"Looks like he's tired," Salazar said. "Anyway, it was nice meeting you. I have an appointment."

He's not the thief, Rosa said. *But he's involved somehow.*

Good to know, Laurie said mentally.

She gave Salazar a dazzling smile. At least she hoped it was dazzling. And a bit ditzy. "We won't keep you." She wondered how she could keep following him. Her car was a few blocks in the other direction now. She could never make it back in time to get in and find him again. Then she remembered the tracking device and gave him a little wave. "Thanks for saving my dog."

Like I needed saving. Rosa stuck her nose in the air.

Of course not. I'm just buttering him up.

Can we get something with butter? Oliver asked.

Laurie shook her head. These canines. She headed back to her Leaf and jumped in. Thumbed on her phone and clicked the tracking icon which Maxwell had designed to look like Sherlock Holme's pipe.

The little red dot moved slowly down Marion Street, then stopped at a Northbean.

Laurie called John at the office. "If I drop the dogs off at Skye's shop, could you come pick them up? Or send someone? Salazar spotted me with them."

"Uh, I guess that's fine. Or I could send Ken."

"Thanks a bunch."

"When will you be back?"

"I'm not sure. Depends on what Salazar does."

"Stay safe."

Laurie called Skye, but it went to voice mail. The store must be busy. Somebody answered at Star, Stone & Flower and Laurie explained the situation.

"Dogs?" Sorcha said.

"I'm following one of the suspects and he spotted them, so—"

"No worries." Sorcha's voice was rushed, the din of customer voices almost drowning her out. "Let me know when you're here and I'll come get them."

"John will pick them up as soon as he can," Laurie said. "Thanks."

"Anything for the cause."

Laurie drove up to Skye's store, darting in and out of lanes on I-5 and listening to Oliver grumble something about not getting any butter. She told him there might be treats at the store, but he had to stay out of the cats' food.

Wild Rose has sharp claws, Rosa said.

True to her word, Sorcha ran out as soon as she saw the Leaf pull into the bus stop. Rosa said she'd sniff out all the customers and Oliver was asking about treats as he lumbered out. Laurie waved goodbye.

Miracles reined and traffic was light on her way back to downtown. At a stop light near Salazar's hotel, she pushed the Sherlock pipe icon and the red dot appeared. She pulled into a garage nearby

—she'd worry about the bill later—and spotted her prey a block away.

Dr. Victor Salazar wandered down First Avenue like a man with nowhere particular to be—hands tucked into the pockets of his rumpled linen jacket, sun hat angled just so to shade his sharp, thoughtful eyes. Except it was cloudy, of course. His gait held that familiar academic looseness: the amble of a man used to dusty trails and museum basements, but equally at home among the curated clutter of urban antique shops.

Laurie watched him from across the street, phone angled low. The little red dot representing him pulsed steadily on her tracking app, right over Old Harbor Curiosities. Perfect.

She ducked behind a rack of Seattle sweatshirts outside a tourist stall as he pushed open the antique shop's door, a bell chiming sharply. Once he disappeared inside, she slipped in after him, letting a couple with giant coffees serve as cover.

The place smelled of beeswax, old leather, and a hint of mildew —the holy trinity of antique shops everywhere. Salazar took his time, drifting from case to case, pausing to admire a brass sextant and a carved obsidian mirror. He murmured something appreciative.

Laurie edged close enough to listen without spooking him. He chatted amiably with the shop owner about the mirror—authentic, probably from Mexico City, late 19th century—but nothing suspicious. Just a collector making small talk. A bored collector at that.

After ten minutes, he left without buying anything.

Laurie exhaled and tapped her screen. The little red dot moved north, toward Pike Place. She leaned against a building and texted Skye.

> LAURIE: You do realize I'm getting my steps in today.

> SKYE: Cardio AND surveillance. Multitasking, babe.

LAURIE: Nothing weird yet. He's just browsing and being extremely… Salazar.

SKYE: Academic or "rogue archaeologist who steals cursed relics" Salazar?

LAURIE: Jury's out.

The dot paused a few blocks up. Laurie spotted him on the patio of *The Black Cormorant Café*, eating clam chowder and a basket of garlic fries like a man who'd finally remembered food existed. He pulled out a notebook—naturally—and jotted something down between bites.

She stayed well out of his line of sight, taking up residence behind a towering potted fern whose fronds did heroic work concealing her.

Her stomach growled.

She sent another message to Skye.

LAURIE: He's having chowder. And fries. And I want both.

SKYE: You're on surveillance, not a lunch date.

LAURIE: I can multitask too.

SKYE: You'll lose him.

LAURIE: He's eating like a man who hasn't seen food since Tuesday. I'd have time for a three-course meal.

Still, she stayed put.

When he finally stood, paid, and drifted off again, she followed —at a distance—down a side street lined with metaphysical and New Age shops.

The tracker dot stilled again.

Laurie looked up.

He'd stepped into Crystals & Curios, a narrow shop glowing with prisms and lit-up amethyst cathedrals. A row of quartz points on the sidewalk sparkled, as if gossiping amongst themselves.

"Well, great," Laurie murmured and slipped inside behind a cluster of tourists.

Salazar stood at the counter, arms folded, studying a display of crystal skull carvings—most of them the size of golf balls and the color of various cocktails.

"Do you carry any skulls from Central America?" he asked, his tone courteous but probing.

The shopkeeper—a woman wearing at least eight rings and a shawl covered in embroidered moons—brightened. "Oh! We get shipments from Oaxaca sometimes. Smaller pieces, mostly."

"I'm looking for something...older." Salazar tapped one of the skulls lightly. "Ever hear about any ancient ones in Seattle?"

Laurie's breath caught.

The shopkeeper's face pinched. "People say all kinds of things. And that woman with the rose quartz skull—she insists it's Atlantean." She rolled her eyes. "Everything I sell comes with provenance. Atlantis does *not* provide paperwork."

Salazar chuckled politely. "Fair enough."

He drifted toward a shelf of smoky quartz tabbies. Laurie followed at a safe distance, pretending to examine a bowl of tumbled stones labeled 'Dragon's Heart Jasper' (which looked suspiciously like regular jasper).

Salazar continued, "Real ancient skulls...they're rare. The truly old ones, even rarer."

The shopkeeper shrugged. "If one were here, trust me, the entire New Age community would have posted about it already."

Salazar hummed as though filing that answer away for later.

Laurie backed toward the exit.

Outside, she tapped her phone.

LAURIE: He asked about ancient skulls.

SKYE: Oh delightful. That's exactly what we needed on this fine day.

LAURIE: The shopkeeper mentioned Celeste's claim that hers is Atlantean.

SKYE: What did she think?

LAURIE: She doesn't believe it. Said if there was an ancient skull in Seattle, the New Agers would be posting about it.

SKYE: But they're not. Ken picked up the dogs, by the way.

LAURIE: Good. Hope they weren't any trouble.

SKYE: Some customers loved them. They behaved.

LAURIE: Think I should I keep following him?

SKYE: Has he met with anyone shady yet?

LAURIE: No. He's just vibing his way through downtown with chowder and crystals.

SKYE: Then maybe shadow him a little longer...but don't get spotted.

Laurie sighed and started after the red dot again as it moved toward another shop. "I'm going to need a foot massage after this," she muttered. But she kept walking. They needed to know what Salazar was after—and whether he was here alone.

Laurie gave him another hour. He visited another New Age store, asked a few leading questions, but the two shopkeepers, dressed as Santa's elves, said they'd never heard of an ancient skull in Seattle. They made him promise to tell them if the rumor was true, saying they'd host an event and pressing their card on him. Salazar smiled and nodded, then made his escape, heading back to his hotel and staying put for another half hour.

Laurie decided he was done wandering around the downtown shops. She swung by her parents' house to pay another visit to Natasha, stroking her and keeping an eye on the little red dot, which stayed put. Then she headed home, put her feet in John's lap (hint, hint), and listened to him talk about his day at work. He massaged her feet as he told her about the plans to free the Skagit River from its dams, but eventually his mind turned to other things and his hands wandered to other places.

CHAPTER

FIFTEEN

Dana had been sitting in her SUV long enough for the heater to cycle through all three stages of "barely warm," "almost cozy," and "now I'm roasting alive." She settled on cracking the window. Cold air drifted in along with strands of fog, carrying the scent of pine and distant saltwater from the Sound.

Her laptop balanced on the console beside her, the glowing screen the only bright thing on this quiet, upscale street. Vale's mansion loomed half-hidden by trees and an ornate iron gate. Christmas lights twinkled innocently over the entrance—red, gold, and warm white. They looked like something from a postcard.

Dana had been around long enough to know that nothing here was innocent.

She pulled her coat tighter, leaned forward, and eyed the live feed Maxwell had patched into her laptop. Two functioning cameras left. One in the central gallery where Vale hosted his soirées. One positioned in a service hallway that looked over the shoulder of a horned Celtic deity.

Maxwell had described it to her. She didn't know enough about

Celtic mythology to know the identity of the god. Honestly, Vale had so many statues and artifacts, he sprinkled them everywhere. Dana wondered if there was one in the kitchen. Some cooking deity.

The dot on a map pulsed in the corner of her screen: Vale's phone tracker. Still at home. Good.

She clicked to enlarge the hallway feed. A long, empty tunnel of polished stone. Muted sconces. Shadows like waiting sentinels. She was getting bored. Laurie was downtown following Salazar today, probably sipping Northbean chai and doing some Christmas shopping on the sly. That sounded more interesting that sitting in her car watching a screen.

"Come on, come on," Dana muttered. "Do something suspicious."

A flicker of motion.

Finally.

Dana's breath hitched as Vale strode into frame, robes sweeping behind him—he'd traded the tailored suit from the party for something darker, looser, heavy with embroidered sigils. His posture was stiff, controlled. He paused in the hallway, raised his hands, and traced glowing runes along the wall. They sank into the stone like drops of molten gold. The entire hallway pulsed once, as if taking a breath.

Dana leaned closer. "Whoa. Must be warding. And it's strong. That's not good."

Skye had warned her that Vale would tighten his magical perimeter. But watching it on screen made her stomach knot. Plus, the fact that she could actually see his sigils, like with her naked eye, surprised the heck out of her. Did it have something to do with the camera lens? Like how cell phones picked up northern lights the naked eye missed?

Vale turned sharply and disappeared through a door—one Dana didn't recognize.

She switched cameras. The central room flickered alive.

Even from the distorted lens angle, the space looked massive.

Arched ceilings. Oil paintings whose subjects seemed to shift when the light caught them wrong. And those black marble floors—once spotless—were now dusted with ritual powders forming an incomplete circle.

He continued warding, tracing sigils in each direction. The dust swirled with his movements. Suddenly, Vale bent down and placed his palms flat on the floor, then shot up, spreading his arms out. Dana gaze jerked away from the computer as golden light spread out, surrounding the house, traveling to the property line, then melting into the fence and ground.

"Blast," Dana whispered. It wasn't the camera, then. She rubbed her eyes. Had he just set some kind of alarm system? Would he know if she crossed this line of gold energy? And why could she see it? Was it like spiritual energy, the same as seeing ghosts? Her gift was growing. Too bad she hadn't gotten a receipt so she could return it.

Dana looked back at her screen. Vale strode into the center of the circle, holding a scroll. He unrolled it with theatrical precision and studied it, muttering to himself.

Dana slid her cursor toward the volume icon. Maxwell had said the audio might cut in and out...but luck was on her side.

Vale's voice came through in jagged fragments.

"...must intersect here..."

"...Fairfax had better..."

"...sun's nadir... the wheel about to turn..."

"...Christmas Eve..."

Dana's pulse spiked. Christmas Eve. Midnight. Fairfax. Ritual. She typed a quick message into her encrypted chat with Maxwell:

> DANA: He's definitely prepping something big. He just said "wheel about to turn." That mean anything?
>
> MAXWELL: Astronomical term. I'll check. Keep watching.

"Like I have a choice," Dana whispered.

A sharp knock against her window nearly made her launch her laptop into the next universe. She froze. Had somebody called the police on her, reporting a suspicious car parked too long in this high-end neighborhood? She eased her gaze left.

A raccoon, a fat one with judgmental eyes, stared at her through the glass. It pawed at the glass.

"I don't have anything for you."

It sighed—*sighed*—and waddled off.

Dana returned to the feed.

Vale was pacing now, chanting under his breath. The camera's microphone picked up only the cadence, not the words—low, rhythmic, something old. Then a tapestry on the wall fluttered. The crystals on the dangling chandelier moved. A breeze swept through the room, though Dana couldn't see any open windows.

A cold shiver prickled down Dana's spine.

Another fifteen minutes passed. Dana squirmed. She needed to pee. Why didn't Vale live next to a strip mall or a Northbean so she could run in and use their facilities? She eyed the salal bush she'd parked next to. She'd hiked with her parents and camped with Kevin. She could do it. Just as she reached for the doorhandle, a stretch limo drove by and turned into the gates of Vale's mansion.

She didn't have to duck because she'd ordered tinted windows. That was back when Kevin was running for office and photographers showed up sticking their cameras in the faces of her kids in their old car. She snapped a picture of the back end of the car and sent it to Maxwell, smiling at the irony. Then she paid the bush a quick visit.

Back in the car, she poked the computer and the central room swam into focus. She saw movement. Not Vale. Someone else stepped into the room.

Dana tapped the zoom.

A man in a dark coat. Nervous. Young, early twenties. Hair slicked back like he was trying too hard. He held a leather satchel tight to his chest. He was *not* part of the staff.

Fairfax? No—too young.

Vale stopped pacing and turned toward his visitor. "Tell me you brought it," Vale said, voice calm but deadly.

"I snuck it out. The Hierophant will excommunicate me if he knows. As we agreed, this settles my debt to you. No more contact." The young man thrust the satchel forward.

"Yes, yes," Vale said impatiently. He snatched the satchel, opened it, and peered inside. A faint blue glow illuminated his face.

Dana strained forward. "What is that?"

Vale smiled—not with joy, but relief. "Finally."

Her skin crawled.

Then the camera fizzled. The screen went black for three seconds. "No, no, no..." Dana slapped the laptop.

The feed reconnected. The young messenger was gone. Vale remained, holding the glowing object close, examining it from every angle. He whispered something that made Dana's stomach flip: "Now all I need is the skull."

Tomorrow was Christmas Eve. And whatever Vale was planning...it had just entered its final phase. Dana reached for her phone to message Maxwell—

Her laptop pinged. The little red dot on her map moved through the house and then began sliding toward the front gate. Fast.

"Oh no," Dana whispered. She snapped her laptop shut, slid it into the passenger seat, and started the SUV's engine.

"Wherever you're going, Vale," she muttered, "I'll be right behind you."

Dana eased her SUV out from behind a row of manicured hedges just as the iron gates of Vale's estate swung open. His black luxury sedan slid out like a shark leaving its cave, headlights cutting sharp white pathways through the winter-dark street.

The day was clear enough to make the Sound glitter in the distance, but the wind was picking up—a thin, sharp edge that scraped across her nerves.

Her phone buzzed on the console. She asked it to read the text and record her answer.

MAXWELL: Where is he going?

DANA: No idea. Just moving. Alone.

MAXWELL: That limo? Registered to an Octavio Lorne.

DANA: Is he this hierophant the guy mentioned?

MAXWELL: Yes, head of the Collegium of the Inner Light. Very secretive. Turns out Vale studied with them years ago.

DANA: So Vale is not just a collector. You're telling me he's a trained magician?

MAXWELL: Looks that way. Found a secret site for elite magical types. His name is listed as a former member of that group.

DANA: All that rigamarole we saw this morning makes sense now. Good to know who we're dealing with.

MAXWELL: Yeah, so be careful.

She flicked a glance to the rearview mirror. Empty street. Good.

Vale's sedan turned left onto the arterial road, heading toward the city. The weather did her a favor; it was that cold, crisp December afternoon right before the holidays when everyone was out doing last-minute shopping or panicking about forgetting batteries. Traffic was messy, chaotic, and blessedly distracting. She let the chaos cloak her.

Her SUV trundled along behind a Subaru with a "Keep Seattle Shroomy" bumper sticker, doing a blessedly slow 28 mph. Vale's sedan quickened its pace. Then, it abruptly changed lanes.

Dana's eyebrows lifted. "Don't even think about stopping, buddy."

He thought about stopping.

Vale's sedan slid into a grocery store lot.

Dana laughed. "You aren't fooling anyone. I know you don't know the price of milk."

Vale parked. And rolled down his driver's window.

She drove past at a very normal, law-abiding speed, eyes forward, resisting the urge to rubberneck. Once she was clear, she turned onto a narrow residential street lined with cypress hedges and parked behind the largest one.

Seconds stretched. A car passed. Another. A jogger in neon green. Dana peered through a gap in the hedge. Vale's silhouette was visible —just barely—leaning out the window, looking...listening.

She held her breath. "Come on," she whispered. "Move."

Finally—*finally*—Vale pulled back onto the road.

Dana pulled out after him, giving him even more distance this time. Enough that she could pretend she wasn't following him even to herself. She followed from roughly six cars back, adjusting lanes, pretending to fight for position like everyone else. Vale's sedan wove through traffic with surgical precision.

Then, abruptly, he cut across two lanes and ducked into the parking entrance beneath a luxurious condo tower Dana recognized —the Pike Place Lofts. Maxwell had discovered Fairfax owned a unit in this building.

Dana followed—but carefully. She didn't enter the garage. Instead, she pulled into a loading zone around the corner and turned her SUV off. Dana stared at the tower entrance.

Cars came and went. The sun sank behind the Cascades. Lights came on all around her.

People walked through the warm golden lobby—residents carrying holiday shopping bags, a dog-walker juggling three leashes, a doorman almost hidden behind an absurdly large poinsettia display. Christmas lights blinked in windows.

And somewhere inside, Adrian Vale was preparing the final steps of a ritual that would happen on Christmas Eve.

CHAPTER

SIXTEEN

Across the city, Maxwell hunched over his workstation—the glow of six monitors painting his face in shifting neon blues and greens. The last surviving camera feed from Dana's laptop crackled with intermittent static, but the frames he needed was intact: Vale lifting the leather satchel and opening it under the chandelier's pale gold light.

Maxwell slowed the footage to a crawl.

Clicked zoom.

Zoomed again.

"Come on, sweetheart," he muttered to the pixels. "Show me your secrets."

The object Vale removed from the bag gave off a gentle blue shimmer, soft as candle flame through frosted glass. The glow pulsed faintly, almost like a slow heartbeat. Maxwell zoomed again and the image cleared. A disk. Palm-sized, crafted from a smooth, moon-pale metal that looked like silver.

Maxwell toggled through enhancement filters. A pattern revealed itself. The surface was engraved with six concentric spirals, each one made of delicate, almost imperceptible lines. He inhaled sharply. "What the –?"

He opened a private site he'd found where magical types asked research questions. It was an elite group. Required completion of at least two full courses in recognized magical orders or mystery schools. Had some gnarly firewalls. All hoity-toity and all, but Maxwell had found a back door. He'd toyed with opening a profile, thinking up appropriate magical names—RuneCipher or SigilByte—but decided against it at the last minute.

He initiated an image search for the disk, keeping his original picture off their site. He let the program run and walked into the kitchen to grab an energy drink in a sleek black can that claimed to enhance "focus, vitality, and algorithmic intuition." Sipping, he watched until the search stopped on an image of the same artifact with an explanation below.

"Bingo," Maxwell shouted and sat to read.

It started with a description, mentioning what Maxwell had already noted on the front side of the disk. Then it continued: "The spirals never quite seem still—if you stare long enough, they feel like they drift, rotate, or breathe, though the disk remains perfectly motionless in your hand.

"The back side is set with three tiny insets of old quartz, cloudy and imperfect, each one holding a faint psychic residue of past mediums who used it. Those crystals warm slightly to the touch when the disk is active and cool again when the connection fades.

"When used properly, it softens the barrier between the user and the spirit world and helps a practitioner attune to subtle emotional signatures lingering in objects or places. It amplifies what is already present, revealing the spiritual connections between the object and the astral, mental, and causal planes."

Maxwell sat back. It looked like Vale was trying to call in some higher-level connection with an object he had. Could it be Anuun? Was he trying to bring in the skull's guiding spirit? For what purpose?

One of the suspects had believed Anuun was attuned to some cosmic being who could bring the earth into alignment. Recreate a golden age. He searched his notes for a few keywords.

Salazar. It was Victor Salazar.

That didn't make sense based on what they'd uncovered so far. Was Salazar connected with the ritual that Vale was planning? What had they missed?

Maxwell sent out an encrypted group message to Dana and her friends telling them what he'd discovered. "Salazar might be connected to Vale more than we've previously suspected."

Soon little icons appeared showing everyone had received the message.

VOLUNTEER PARK GLOWED like a lantern against the early winter dark. Strings of golden lights hung from the trees, swaying gently in the cold breeze. Luminaries lined the paths, guiding people toward the open field where Celeste Ardolf had erected her Solstice circle—a towering bonfire stacked with care, evergreen boughs laid around it in a spiral. Drummers warmed up on the far side, a low heartbeat rumbling through the earth.

Laurie walked in with John at her side, Rosa and Oliver trotting ahead in reflective vests Skye had insisted on. Minh jogged to catch up, cheeks pink from the cold. Hoa—eyes bright with excitement— ran straight toward a booth selling holly crowns. Skye and Jade followed more slowly, appreciating the ambience.

"This is gorgeous," Skye murmured. "Celeste really outdid herself."

"It's the solstice," Jade said. "Of course she did."

Wild costumes swirled around them—fae wings made of fiber optics, horned headdresses, cloaks with embroidered constellations. One man was painted blue and carried a cardboard moon. A trio of women wore sunburst masks and jingling belts. Rosa sniffed them all, delighted. Oliver bumped her gently with his shoulder so the little Havanese didn't get too tangled in a woman's trailing ribbons.

Above the murmur of voices, Celeste stepped into the center of the circle, raising her arms. She wore a cloak of deep forest green, her silver-blonde hair braided with winter jasmine.

"Welcome all," she called, her voice projecting effortlessly. "Tonight, we celebrate the longest night—and the promise of the sun's return."

The crowd hushed.

"The solstice is our reminder that even in our darkest moments, light waits just beyond the horizon. The sun stands still for three days and on Christmas morning, begins to move forward again."

A rotund man dressed as the Holly King came forward to stand by her side. Was that Dr. Lucien Harrow, Laurie wondered. The man who'd spilled the beans to Ravenna? If so, he must have padded his stomach for his costume tonight. She looked around for the elementary school teacher, but the crowd was too big to spot her.

"If you've written your intentions for the coming year, hold them now." She lit the bonfire with a flourish—blue fire catching, then flaring gold.

"I hope she has a permit for that fire," Jade said.

Skye patted her arm. "You're not on duty tonight."

Gasps and cheers rang out. "When you're ready, throw your intentions into the flames with a wish for them to grow as the days lengthen. If you didn't write them down," she added with a warm smile, "simply stand before the fire. Think about what you'd like to see flourish in your life this year. Speak from the heart. The fire will hear you."

Laurie looked over at John. "Did you write anything?"

He tapped a folded paper in his pocket. "Figured it couldn't hurt."

"I didn't," Laurie admitted.

Rosa sat at her feet. *I intend to get more chicken in the coming year,* she informed her hopefully.

Laurie snorted. *We'll work on that.*

The drummers struck up a rhythm, and the crowd began swirling around the fire—dancing, laughing, casting shadows that leapt and twisted. Hoa and Minh joined in immediately, spinning hand in hand. Jade clapped along. Skye took photos, already planning a solstice display for Star, Stone & Flower.

Near the edge of the circle, Laurie spotted Victor Salazar. She pulled her floppy hat down low over her face.

He had foregone his usual hat and instead wore a thick scarf and a vaguely Mayan-patterned coat. He stood with his hands tucked behind his back, surveying the festivities with academic interest—and a touch of genuine wonder.

Before Laurie could drift closer, Celeste approached him.

Laurie caught Skye's sleeve. "There. Come on."

Jade guided Oliver and Rosa to sit near a stone bench. The dogs obeyed, though Rosa kept jumping up, wanting to go play with the dancers.

Laurie and Skye lingered near a temporary art installation—a large wire-and-glass sculpture of a phoenix—pretending to take photos. They weren't the only ones. Half the crowd was occupied with enthusiastic pretending.

Celeste lowered her voice. "Dr. Salazar. I'm glad you came."

"I'm always pleased to witness solstice traditions in new places," he replied. "Seattle has its own flavor."

Celeste studied him a moment, then stepped a little closer. "You asked me about old crystal skulls."

His brows lifted. "Yes. I've been following the rumors. You know I've spent decades studying the old Mesoamerican pieces."

"Well," she said delicately, "I should tell you...the ancient skull recently in Seattle—the one tied to Atlantean artifacts. It's been stolen."

Salazar's surprise was immediate. "Stolen? When?"

"Very recently." She folded her arms. "Now would be an ideal time for us to find it."

"Interesting way of putting it," Laurie whispered in Skye's ear.

Salazar studied Celeste, eyebrows drawn together over sharp eyes. He didn't respond immediately, so she stumbled to add, "Before it comes to harm."

He nodded grimly. "I agree. Such an artifact could be...dangerous in the wrong hands."

Laurie felt Skye tense beside her. What had he been going to say before he hesitated?

Celeste continued, "We don't know who took it yet."

Salazar frowned. "Then whoever has it is either reckless or skilled. Neither is encouraging."

The two spoke a little longer, too low for Laurie and Skye to catch more. When Celeste drifted away to greet a family in antler crowns, Salazar walked closer to the fire and stared into it a long moment, worry etched across his face.

Laurie exhaled. "Well. That was a whole mood."

Skye crossed her arms. "Celeste knows Salazar. She told him about the theft."

"He seemed surprised," Laurie said. "What did you pick up?"

"His surprise was genuine," Skye said.

Lauri trusted her empathic friend.

"I don't know what to make of that given Maxwell's last message," Skye said.

Minh and Hoa danced past them in a whirlwind of scarves and laughter.

Laurie smiled, watching the teens romp like younger children. "I don't think we'll discover anything more tonight. We'll know where they both go after this. Maybe we can relax a little. Enjoy all this."

Skye's expression softened. "Solstice reminds us the light always comes back."

"Maybe Anuun will, too," Laurie said.

Jade waved them toward the fire. "Come on! Toss your intentions!"

Laurie looked at Minh, at Hoa's smile, at the fire blooming gold against the dark. She stepped forward to join her friends, her dogs, and the thrum of drums lifting her heart.

The world was still in chaos—but for tonight, there was warmth. There was community. And there was hope that they could find Anuun and bring him to safety.

CHAPTER

SEVENTEEN

Christmas Eve dawned bright, the kind of pale winter gold that made the frosted rooftops sparkle. A hush hung over Capitol Hill, the stillness carrying a promise that snow might drift in later—soft, slow, storybook flakes.

Inside Dana's kitchen, however, the world was anything but peaceful. Spiced steam curled up from the griddle, carrying cinnamon and cardamom into every corner like a festive enchantment. The old Victorian seemed to sigh contentedly under the buttery warmth.

Dana flipped another pancake, the edges crisping just right, and slid it onto the growing tower on Minh's plate.

"Seriously? You're planning on eating all those?" She brandished her spatula at the stack.

"I'm still a growing boy, Mom." Minh winked, his grin pure mischief.

"You're a college student and budding hacker is what you are," she shot back, the corners of her mouth betraying her amusement.

"I'm only eating four," Hoa declared primly. She lifted her fork with a dramatic, delicate poise that would have made any runway model proud.

Dana sighed inwardly. With her opalescent skin and cheekbones sharp enough to cut glass, Hoa was becoming painfully beautiful. Fortunately, her daughter remained blissfully unaware, more focused on pancakes than fashion empires, unlike Nicolette Voss, Kevin's former campaign stylist, current "companion."

"Is the plan still on for you to spend today with your father?" Dana asked, sliding another pancake onto a plate.

"Nah," Minh said around a mouthful so large it should've been criminal.

Dana leveled a look at him.

He froze, cheeks bulging, while Hoa rescued him without missing a beat. "Dad and Nicolette suddenly flew off to Vail."

Minh swallowed triumphantly. "Got an invitation from some celebrity who has a ranch in them there hills."

Dana laughed, a bright spark in the warm kitchen. "I don't think 'them there hills' quite matches the glittering inhabitants of those mountains. I'm sorry your plans got changed at the last minute."

"We're not," the kids chimed together.

Dana paused mid-flip. "Really? Why not?"

"We'd rather hang out at the farm," Hoa said. "Isn't that where we're going tonight?"

Minh waggled his eyebrows—an attempt at villainy that landed somewhere between cartoonish and adorable. "Aren't you in the middle of an investigation?"

"If you're father's gone, we'll spend some time with your grandparents. Presents, then an afternoon candlelight service at their church." Dana picked up her phone to call them. They never read their texts.

Hoa looked at Minh. "Think they'll get us outfits for school again?"

"Probably," he said.

Both teens looked dejected.

Dana drew in a sharp breath. "Your grandparents risked their lives—"

"Here comes the speech," Minh whispered, but Dana heard him. She planted her hands on her hips. "It's true. They escaped a terrible war. Your grandfather lost most of his family. They didn't have—"

The teens joined in and finished the sentence with her, "clothes for school."

"We know, Mom," Hoa said, managing to sound apologetic.

"Minh, you take Hoa in your new car," Dana said.

"New? You call your old 2018 Honda new?"

"Your grandparents—"

Minh threw up his hands. "Okay, okay. I surrender. I love my brand-new Honda."

"After presents, we'll all go to the service, then you can drive out to the farm. I'm going spend a few hours catching up on work. I have an actual job I've been neglecting."

"Mom, something's burning!" Hoa pointed.

Dana whirled back to the stove and flipped the pancake. A dark stripe ran across its center. "It's only a little burned. I can scrape it off."

"Eew," Hoa groaned.

"I'll eat it." Dana put the last pancake on her plate and took her seat at the island. She up ended the maple syrup, but nothing came out. "Who used all the syrup?"

Lele jumped up on the island just in time to save the kids, looking around for chicken sausage. Dana grabbed the cat's treat from the frying pan and cut it up for her. She put the small plate of sausage on the island in Kevin's old place. Served him right. When she sat back down, she found her pancakes had mysteriously been graced with syrup. She looked up, but both her children were chewing madly and avoiding eye contact.

Dana took her last bite and set her fork down. "Rinse your dishes and put them in the dishwasher." The kids scrambled, bumping shoulders in their rush. Dana cleaned up the rest of the breakfast prep, then topped off Lele's food and water.

"Grab what you'll need for tonight," she called to the kids.

The cat brushed her leg with a low purr, tail curling like a question mark.

"Are we coming home?" Hoa called from her room.

Lele wound around Dana's calves. "We'll try. But bring pj's and toothbrushes just in case."

"We won't abandon you," she whispered to the feline.

Minutes later they piled into their cars, puffing little clouds of breath into the chilly air. Dana fired up her engine as a faint flurry fluttered across the windshield—snow beginning its shy approach. She followed Minh, willing herself to be patient. Her parents looked forward to an afternoon with the kids. She glanced at the tracking app on her phone. The red dots were all stationary, blinking innocently.

Yeah, right, Dana thought.

Thankfully, the suspects were staying put for now. But what miscreants were visiting Vale, she wondered.

Minh's mother had prepared a feast for lunch—spicy beef noodle soup, bánh chung, and spring rolls. Pillow cakes for dessert. Dana eyed Minh as he took second helpings. How did he stuff all that food in and stay the same size? The kids were polite about their new clothes, if not enthusiastic, and they all trundled off to the candle-light service. Her parents like to experience the traditions of their new country. The snow still drifted down, but nothing was sticking yet. Dana stayed behind her parents' car just in case they slid.

St. Ignatius glowed with soft golden light, every arch wrapped in evergreen boughs and red ribbon. Candles clustered near the altar flickered like tiny hearth fires, casting halos across the stained-glass nativity. Incense drifted through the high rafters—Frankincense and myrrh, traditionally soothing, though tonight they only made Dana more aware of her tight shoulders.

Minh slid into the pew first, already taller than his grandfather and growing by the week. Hoa followed, smoothing the skirt of her velvet dress with a seriousness far too mature for fourteen. Dana's mother, Khiem, leaned close to whisper a gentle reminder, "We are here for peace this afternoon, con gái. Let your heart rest."

If only.

Dana sat between her parents and her children, hands clenched in her lap. Her phone—turn off your phone, she reminded herself—was deep in her purse, locked away like a restless spirit. She could feel the weight of all the things she *should* be doing tugging at her: notes for Senator Whitmore, messages from Maxwell, half-written proposals waiting at home on her laptop. And under all of that, a sharper, more mystical anxiety: Where was Anuun now? What was Vale up to?

Beside her, Trong adjusted his glasses and murmured, "You look like you're about to bolt, Dana."

She startled. "I'm fine."

"You're vibrating," Minh whispered with a grin, nudging her shoulder. "Like Rosa before she gets the zoomies."

Hoa elbowed him. "Mom's allowed to be stressed. It's the holidays."

"And she needs a break," Khiem added, giving Dana's hand a quiet squeeze. "This afternoon is for family. The world will wait until after Christmas."

If only that were true. Dana inhaled slowly.

The choir began "O Come, O Come, Emmanuel," voices rising in a haunting minor chord that shivered along her skin. The candles reflected in the polished pew backs, little stars flickering in rows. Children in angel costumes lined up for the procession, wings rustling softly.

It *was* beautiful. It *was* peaceful.

And she was still calculating the fastest route out of the parking lot the second Mass ended.

The priest stepped up for the homily, speaking of the birth of the

Christ child, the promise of redemption, the need for love in these difficult times. People shifted, settled, breathed easier.

Dana tried. She really did. But all she could think about was Vale drawing sigils in the air that she could see by some miracle and the mysterious ritual he had planned for tonight. Probably the opposite of what the priest was talking about.

The final hymn faded into the high rafters, candles guttering in their brass holders as parishioners shuffled out into the cold night. Dana forced herself not to power-walk up the aisle. Her parents moved at their usual ceremonial pace—small steps, polite nods, stopping twice to greet old family friends. Dana matched them, outwardly serene, inwardly coiled like a spring.

In the narthex, they exchanged hugs layered with the lingering scent of frankincense and myrrh.

"New Year's, yes?" Khiem said, cupping Dana's cheek.

"Of course," Dana managed.

"Drive carefully," Trong added, eyes sharp as if he already suspected she was about to do the opposite. "And you as well," he said to Minh.

"Bye, grandpa," Minh said.

Hoa kissed their cheeks and they headed to the incredibly old Honda.

The moment Dana slid into the driver's seat of her SUV, she shut the door, exhaled hard, and thumbed her phone awake.

It chirped—Maxwell's special alert, the one that sounded like a submarine hunting something deep and dangerous.

Her notifications lit up.

> MAXWELL: Salazar is on the move.
>
> SKYE: I'm in the store. Who can tail him?
>
> LAURIE: We just arrived at John's parents.
>
> DANA: On it.

Senator Whitmore's stack of work—drafts, notes, last-minute edits—would have to wait. She tapped the tracking app and watched the red dot drift down a street grid.

Dana threw the SUV into gear and eased out of the lot. Snowflakes spiraled in the glow of the streetlights, catching like silver sparks in her rearview mirror. Salazar's dot paused...then accelerated north.

"Oh, come on," she muttered, turning toward I-5 and merging fast.

Traffic thickened with holiday travelers. Dana wove between cars, trying to remember the rental details—black Volvo? Honda? Something boxy? Her mental files blurred. She risked a speeding ticket, darting into the outside lane. Once she got around a prehistoric sedan sputtering at fifty, she checked the dot just in time to see it exit near Edmonds.

Her gut clenched. Vale's property.

They had practically cleared Salazar this afternoon. Then Maxwell sent that cryptic message—*I think we missed something*—and now this.

"Call Maxwell," she instructed her car's AI.

Maxwell picked up on the first half-ring. "I see it," he said, fingers clacking faintly over keys in the background.

Dana switched lanes to avoid a van drifting like a drunk reindeer. "Good. I need more than cryptic warnings. What did you find last night about Salazar? You never explained."

A pause. Not hesitation—more like him choosing where to start. "You remember the blue-glowing artifact the young man delivered?" he said.

"The one that he stole from his magical lodge? What about it?"

"It's a Harmonic Conductor Disk." Maxwell exhaled sharply, the sound staticky and irritated.

"A what?"

"An ancient tech designed to link physical objects with their counterparts on the higher planes. Think…spiritual Wi-Fi but calibrated for artifacts with sentience or guardians."

Dana's stomach tightened. "Anuun."

"Exactly." She could picture him pushing his glasses up the bridge of his nose. "Vale isn't interested in the skull for research, money, or bragging rights. He's trying to pull in the guide connected to Anuun. The one that exists on the non-physical side."

"His…guide?" Dana said, almost swerving as sleet tapped against the windshield. "As in a spirit being?"

"Not a ghost," Maxwell clarified quickly. "More like a caretaker. A consciousness tied to the skull since its creation. If Vale activates that disk with Anuun nearby, he could bridge the realms long enough to draw the guide into this plane."

Dana felt a cold ripple crawl up her spine. "Why would he want that?"

"Oh, I don't know," Maxwell said dryly. "To control an ancient multidimensional being? To weaponize knowledge humans were never meant to touch? Pick a megalomaniac motive."

Dana tightened her grip on the wheel. "So Salazar going there tonight—"

"—means Vale might be ready to activate the disk. You're going to want eyes on this, Dana. Trust me."

"I always do," she muttered. "Are your cameras still working?"

He snorted. "Of course, but you'll need to be within a couple miles to see anything."

"I've got a good spot near his house."

"I'll be monitoring the feed."

Dana ended the call, pulse hammering, and sped into the twisty shoreline roads—now knowing far more than she wanted to. Fog rose from the shoreline, low and glimmering. When she rounded a tight corner, red taillights flashed ahead—a sleek black Volvo rolling toward Vale's massive iron gate.

Dana killed her headlights and coasted to the familiar clump of salal bushes. She tucked her SUV beneath the sweeping cedar boughs until she was swallowed by shadow.

The gate swallowed the Volvo. Clanged shut behind it.

Dana grabbed her laptop, flipped it open, and loaded Maxwell's interface. Two windows blinked to life—the upstairs corridor and the grand salon. The feed wavered, then sharpened.

Salazar entered the salon, peeling off his fedora. Under his parka he wore a tweed jacket coat and cords, looking very much like the professor he used to be. Vale, dressed in expensive sweats, lounged like royalty mid-break.

Dana raised the volume.

"Victor, it's been quite some time," Vale purred.

"A few years at least," Salazar replied, jaw tight.

Dana leaned closer as the men settled—Vale looking casual, Salazar perched on the edge of his chair like a wolf about to spring. They didn't look like conspirators to Dana. More like opponents.

"I've been following the trail of an artifact," Salazar said. "It led me to Seattle."

Vale lifted a brow. "Tell me about it."

"I think you already know," Salazar said flatly.

Vale adopted a mask of confusion—convincing to anyone who didn't know he collected metaphysical contraband. "I haven't added anything to my collection recently."

"You didn't steal the skull?"

Vale stilled.

Dana zoomed in, heart climbing her ribs. Footsteps. Movement. In the hallway behind Salazar—men in black jackets sweeping past the camera.

"Skull?" Vale echoed, tone sharpening. "What kind?"

"Oh, cut the crap, Adrian" Salazar growled. "You found him. You found the Pure One and you stole him."

"Pure—?"

"You sent that thief of a cousin to that witch's store. You trained

Fairfax to pick locks, open safes, turn off security systems. You getting too old for all that?"

Vale's face flushed. "There's no need to be rude. You're getting rather long in the tooth yourself."

"That skull is uncorrupted by blood sacrifices. We know it is meant to reawaken the master skulls around the world. To bring an end to all this chaos in the world. This is the season for peace on earth."

Vale sat straight, looking regal. "That crystalline network was meant to restore rule to the spiritual elite. Not the corrupt priests of Rome, but those who hold real power. We empower the aristocracy, direct their actions. That is what will bring order to the world. A firm hand backed up by the knowledge of how to handle elemental energy."

"No. The time for that way has passed. We've entered the Age of Aquarius. Spiritual knowledge passes to everyone now."

"The old dream of democracy. But you see where it has gotten us."

Salazar surged to his feet. "Where have you hidden him?"

Vale lifted a single hand.

Four men rushed in like a trap snapping shut. They grabbed Salazar—two at the arms, one bracing his back, the last drawing a pistol.

"You should know better than to threaten me in my own home," Vale said, voice knife edged. "Take him."

Salazar struggled, but the guards held him firm. "What are you—"

"I don't have time for you, Victor. Not today of all days."

Dana's pulse roared in her ears.

Then the feed jerked—the salon scene cutting to static. The hallway view flickered, then caught the men dragging Salazar toward the far end of the corridor.

"Damn it," Dana hissed, shoving her laptop aside.

CHAPTER

EIGHTEEN

Dana cracked her door open and slipped out into the cold night. Snow whispered across the gravel. Beyond the iron gate, the Volvo remained parked, engine cold. But the men were on foot, hauling Salazar deeper into the estate.

She skirted the perimeter until she reached the old service easement—a narrow gap between the fence posts where a storm-tilted cedar had once fallen. The break was still wide enough for someone determined.

Dana dropped to her stomach, crawled under, and popped up on the other side, brushing needles from her coat.

Lights glowed in Vale's windows—warm, opulent, unaware of the shadows slipping around its edges.

Dana stalked along the hedgerow, breath fogging, ears pricked for footsteps. She circled toward the back, where the property sloped into a stand of dark fir trees. The men's voices drifted faintly ahead—muffled grunts, Salazar protesting, boots crunching frozen ground.

She followed.

Beyond the trees, something materialized out of the darkness—a building she had never seen before. A low, rectangular stone—chapel. That was the only word for it. A steeple rose from the roof with a brass figure at the top. A carved wooden door gleamed under a curved awning. Dana couldn't make out any details of the carving.

In contrast to this serene structure, a modern keypad threw off a dull red glow. The armed man punched in a code and the rest shoved Salazar inside. The door slammed.

Dana eased behind a mossy retaining wall, watching the last man disappear inside the bunker-like structure. Snow muffled everything—sound, movement, even her own breathing. She slipped her phone from her coat, thumbed the screen on—

No service.

No bars.

Nothing.

"What—?" She turned in a slow circle. Vale's property was massive, but even out here she should have a sliver of reception. The phone stubbornly displayed *SOS Only*, the battery icon glowing like a taunt.

She opened Maxwell's camera app anyway.

A spinning wheel appeared. Then: *No connection. Feed unavailable.*

"Great," Dana muttered. "Just perfect."

Maxwell had warned her the cameras wouldn't penetrate more than a couple miles. And this—this chapel wasn't on any blueprint. Whatever shielding Vale had built into it, electronic signals didn't stand a chance.

Which meant no one was watching. No one knew where she was. And no one could find her.

A shiver scraped down her spine harder than the winter wind.

She slid the useless phone back into her pocket and crept toward the wooden door. A sliver of light glowed beneath it. She studied the keypad, feeling the faint static hum of electricity powering Vale's custom security tech.

"Okay, Dana," she whispered to herself. "You got yourself into this. Time to get yourself out."

She lifted the small screwdriver from her pocket kit and popped the keypad casing loose with practiced ease. A spark snapped. The security light flickered.

After a tense second—click. The door unlatched.

Dana glanced once over her shoulder at the empty, snow-blanketed woods, then slipped inside the shadows, alone and unseen. The door sighed shut behind her, sealing the outside world away with a solid thud. She stood still for a moment, letting her eyes adjust to the dim, subterranean corridor. No hum of electronics here. No pings from Maxwell's feed. No faint buzz of her phone searching for a tower.

Just her.

Alone.

And the soft, unsettling whisper of warm air moving through stone.

She crept forward.

The hallway sloped downward, its walls narrowing. Recessed sconces sputtered every twenty feet, their amber glow too weak to reach the floor. Shadows pooled thickly at her ankles.

Dana swallowed the knot forming in her throat. "This is fine," she murmured, voice thin. "Stupid, reckless, wildly irresponsible... but fine."

The corridor opened without warning into a cavernous room.

Dana froze.

A cold sweep of air brushed past her, though nothing visible moved. Her breath caught in her chest, her heartbeat pounding so loudly she thought it might echo off the stone.

Two rows of towering statues flanked a central aisle, each figure frozen in mid-myth—gods, guardians, destroyers, protectors. As Dana stepped forward, the carvings loomed above her, their faces half-shadow, half-sculpted divinity.

A rapid ch-ch-ch-ch vibrated from the shadows, the distinct sound of a rattlesnake. Dana froze and studied the ground. She tried the flashlight on her phone, but it didn't work. Two fanged faces peered at her from around the neck of a goddess' face.

Dana risked another step. The rattling stopped. With her next step, the slither of scales against rock reached her ears. Looking up, she saw Medusa, serpents curling out from her head in eternal warning. Was she hearing the power of the statues?

On the next step, bleeding bodies lay all around her. Headless. Looking up, the goddess Kali's stone eyes glinted with harsh, ancient judgment.

She moved forward and was suddenly surrounded by ghosts. But not the kind she was used to. These murmured, pulled at her cloths, hands out. Then she could make out words. "A coin for passage. Please give us passage." She looked up and saw Hades. His cloak seemed almost to shift at the edges. Steeling herself, she took another step and the crowd disappeared.

Was this some kind of demonic gauntlet? Each step brought a new terror. Then it dawned on her. This was the place from Skye's dream. Just as she'd described it. Down to the curvature of the ornate archway and the black basalt floor that shimmered faintly under the sconces.

Dana stopped breathing entirely when she realized the air had changed—not just humid but charged, humming softly in her bones like the moment before lightning strikes.

"Skye was right," she whispered, voice shaking. "Oh, God."

She moved down the aisle, feet silent on the polished stone. The statues towered higher with every step, watching, threatening. She pushed through the apparitions. The chamber seeming to expand around her. At the far end, she saw it—

A dark pedestal.

A soft glow.

A face shining in the dark.

Anuun.

The crystal skull pulsed with inner luminescence, as though aware—awake. The glow cast fractured rainbows on the nearest statue, shimmering over its stone feet.

Dana, at last we meet.

His voice gently brushed against her mind. A wave of love washed over her. Peace settled in her heart.

Dana inhaled sharply, the emotions catching her off guard. The terror, the dread of the chamber melted away.

The crystal shimmered like light turned into sound. An almost imperceptible singing wafted through the space. A pure, bell-like harmony swelled, each note glowing with warmth. A vast chord rose, deep and bright, like galaxies humming in perfect alignment.

Dana's hands flew to her chest. She gasped in wonder.

The angels have been keeping me company in this dark chapel.

"Anuun?" she breathed, stepping closer. "I'm here. I've come to—"

A hand clamped over her mouth.

Another hand seized her arms, wrenching them behind her back. Pain shot down her shoulders. She kicked back, heel connecting with something solid, heard a grunt—but her attacker didn't loosen their grip.

A second figure grabbed her legs. A third yanked a hood over her head, plunging her into suffocating darkness.

"Got her," someone growled in her ear.

Her phone skittered across the basalt floor as they dragged her backward—away from Anuun, away from everything she'd come for. Her boots scraped stone, the statues passing by as indistinct black voids behind the hood.

"No—no!" Dana fought, but her captors' grips tightened like vises.

They hauled her down a sloping passage she hadn't seen, the temperature dropping with each step. Doors clanged open. Metal echoed. Someone shoved her hard. She stumbled down a short flight of stairs, caught by rough hands, thrown again.

Her knees hit cold stone.

Then—

SLAM.

A heavy door locked, the reverberation vibrating through her ribs.

Silence.

CHAPTER

NINETEEN

J ade handed Skye a small velvet box, the deep crimson fabric
catching the glow of the hearth. Their tiny house felt especially
magical tonight—tree twinkling in the corner, strings of faery
lights climbing the curtain rods like luminous vines and the
tops of the bookcases shimmering with soft golden halos. Pillar
candles flickered in a loose circle on the coffee table, their warm light
dancing across shelves of crystals and herb jars.

Gandalf was curled on his pillow near the fire, tail wrapped
neatly around him like a regal plume. Ashe and Taran lay sprawled
on the rug, enormous treats clamped between their paws, their
synchronized gnawing keeping imperfect rhythm with the Celtic
Christmas music drifting through the room.

"Oh my," Skye whispered, turning the little velvet box over in her
palm. "This *looks* expensive."

"Open it," Jade said, practically vibrating with anticipation.

Skye closed her eyes for a moment, letting the emotion radiating
from her wife flow through her—warm, fizzing, expectant. Whatever
sat inside this box made Jade happy. That alone made Skye nervous
in the best way. She opened the lid.

A row of small diamonds winked back at her from a slender band of white gold, scattering prismatic sparks across her fingers.

"What is this?" she breathed. She lifted the ring free, heart thumping. "You want to marry me again?"

Jade laughed, the sound low and rich, warming Skye in all the ways that mattered. "No, mon cher. I just want all those women who flirt with you in the U-District to know you're very much taken."

"But I didn't get *you* one." Skye's voice came out softer than she intended.

"I don't want to have to explain a wedding band to some of the cops," Jade said dryly. "They'd be... less than kind." She took the ring gently from Skye's hand and slipped it onto her finger, saying the same words she'd said at their wedding. "May our love flourish, nurture, and guide us."

Skye bent in, kissed her, and heat surged between them—golden, rising, inevitable. And then, right on cue, her phone shrilled.

They broke apart with a groan and a laugh. Skye fished for the phone, saw her mother's name blazing across the screen, and answered with: "What do you need now?"

Her mother didn't bother with greetings. "We need you two. Are you coming? It's time to light the tree, and we can't hold off the young ones any longer."

Snow fell thickly as Skye and Jade made their way up the path toward the big Yarrow house, each flake catching in Skye's scarf like a tiny star. Ashe and Taran bounded ahead, kicking up white plumes, yipping as if the snow itself were a blessing. Through the frost-rimmed windows, golden light spilled out in welcome.

Inside was cheerful pandemonium. Pots and pans steamed on the stove; rosemary and thyme drifted from the roasting turkey; the unmistakable scent of freshly risen bread warmed the air.

The front door flew open behind them with a burst of cold wind. Laurie and John stumbled in, arms overloaded with presents. Rosa and Oliver barreled through their legs with delighted barks, Ashe and Taran giving chase.

"Sorry we're late," Laurie said, shaking off snowflakes. "I had to drive. John still hasn't learned to drive in snow."

"Welcome," Cormac said, clapping John on the back. "You didn't need bring all this."

"Yes, we did," Laurie insisted. "Your family has done so much for us."

Two-year-old Ian spotted Skye and immediately launched into a bounce-dance. "Tree lights! Tree lights!" He latched onto her hand and tried to tug her toward the living room.

"We have to bring back the light!" five-year-old Fiadh called from across the room, already vibrating with anticipation.

"It looks like we're just in time," John said.

The front room overflowed with Yarrows—people sitting on the floor, leaning against furniture, perched on arms of chairs. Minh and Hoa huddled with the cluster of teens; the littlest ones fidgeted in a loose sea of excitement at the base of the towering Douglas fir.

"Settle down," Fíona urged. "Our storyteller is ready."

"Tree lights," Ian reminded helpfully.

Uncle Ewan stepped up, hands dramatically clasped. "Now then," he said. "We've already celebrated solstice night. Do you remember what happens then?"

"We light candles!"

"We eat lots of food!"

The children shouted their favorite parts. Laughter rippled through the room.

"On winter solstice," Ewan continued, widening his eyes in mock fright, "our ancestors worried the sun might never return."

"No..." Fiadh whispered, terrified and delighted.

"So they lit candles and burned logs and decorated the mother tree. And after three long nights, what happens?"

"Baby Jesus," Sinead murmured, hugging herself.

"And the days grow longer. The sun returns. Light comes back into the world. What better time for the world teacher to be born—the one who brings peace and hope?"

Ian plopped down in front of Ewan, thumb instantly in his mouth.

"And how do we celebrate?"

"We light the tree!" every child shrieked.

Ronan plugged in the cord. The fir blazed to life, ornaments flashing like captured stars. The room erupted in cheers. Ian tipped his head back in awe, tiny mouth forming a perfect O.

"The wheel has turned," Ewan declared.

"Presents! Presents!"

Fíona began handing out brightly wrapped boxes as the room erupted into organized chaos. Laurie and John emerged from the kitchen carrying their own stack.

"Skye, this one's for you," Laurie said. "Jade—here."

They took the packages with warm smiles. "Yours under the tree —" Jade looked at the mound still piled there "—somewhere."

"Dana, here's—" Laurie paused. "Where's Dana?"

"Dana?" John called toward the kitchen.

At that exact moment, Laurie's and Skye's phones chimed in unison—the distinctive tone Maxwell reserved for emergencies.

They exchanged a glance and lifted their screens. A new message blinked up from Maxwell: *Dana has disappeared. I think Vale has her.*

The room around them blurred into background noise. The cozy warmth of the tree vanished beneath a sharp spike of fear.

Just as Laurie started to reply, a new text appeared: *Vale's cameras caught her sneaking onto his property.*

A map thumbnail appeared. Then a video clip. *See attached.*

Skye tapped the video. Grainy night footage resolved into Dana —crawling under a chain-link fence, snow clinging to her coat, breath puffing white. The camera followed her until the image cut off abruptly.

"Oh goddess," Skye whispered.

Laurie sucked in a breath, color draining from her face. "She went alone."

Jade's hand closed around Skye's arm, steady and sure. "She's alive in that video. That's something."

The laughter of the room evaporated. One by one, conversations faltered. Heads lifted. The Yarrow clan were many things—rowdy, magical, loud—but when danger stalked one of their own, they shifted in perfect synchrony.

Cormac moved first, his expression sharpening as he stepped closer. "What's happened?"

Skye held up her phone so he could see the message. "Dana's missing. Vale has her. Maxwell got camera footage."

"One of the men you think stole Anuun?" her father asked.

"Yes."

"I thought she was tracking Salazar," Laurie said.

"Maybe they're working together," Skye said.

Fíona was already clearing space on the big coffee table, sweeping aside wrapping paper and half-opened gifts. "Maps. Get the maps up."

Ronan lunged for the remote and switched the TV input. "Airdrop it," he said. "Let's get eyes on the property."

The teens—usually half-feral with holiday excitement—snapped to attention. Minh stepped forward, cool and focused. "If she went in on foot, we need to look at heat signatures, blind spots, anything."

"I can help," Hoa said, pulling out her tablet. "Maxwell may send more data."

Fíona herded the younger kids toward the kitchen. "Upstairs for cocoa, all of you. This is grown-up business now. Go. Move."

Uncle Ewan stood beside the mantle, arms crossed, gaze fierce. "If Vale's touched a hair on that woman's head..."

"We're not starting a war tonight," Fíona warned, though her voice trembled with controlled fury. "Not until we know exactly where she is."

The big screen flickered, loading Maxwell's satellite map. A cluster of red dots marked Vale's sprawling property: house, security outbuildings, and a blank spot—right where Dana had disappeared on the footage.

Laurie's jaw set. "That's where she went dark."

Jade leaned in, eyes narrowing. "Maybe a hidden structure. Probably where he'd take her."

Cormac grunted. "Then that's where we go."

Skye grabbed Jade's hand and squeezed once—hard—before stepping closer to the screen. "We find her. Tonight. Before Vale does anything else."

Minh nodded solemnly. "Maxwell's typing." His phone buzzed. "He says he's trying to get into Vale's internal security feed. He'll send anything he finds."

"Good," Laurie said, breath shaky but resolve forming like steel. "We go now. We're not waiting."

Skye chased a single lungful of air and let it out slowly. The mother tree still glowed in the corner, lights sparkling as if unaware the night had turned.

The Yarrow clan shifted into a familiar ancestral rhythm—older than their farm, older than the family house, older even than any holiday tradition they held dear.

Cormac didn't raise his voice. He didn't need to. "Findlay. Tadhg. Eamon."

Three heads snapped up at once.

Findlay—tall, broad-shouldered, a quiet wall of reliability—set down the plate of shortbread he'd been holding and strode toward the coat hooks.

Tadhg, the weather witch, was already halfway to the mudroom. "On it."

Eamon, steady and thoughtful, stood from the armchair and rolled up his sleeves. "What do we need?"

"Winter kits. All of them." Cormac's tone meant no delays. "And bring the ironwood staff."

Skye felt the air change around her—the energy thickening,

crackling like static before a storm. The Yarrows didn't scramble. They *mobilized*.

Mateo stepped forward. "You're going to need a shapeshifter."

Grandmother Moira paused on the first step of the stairs, a big tin of cookies in one hand. "Aye, he'll come in handy, that one."

Cormac nodded his approval.

Findlay returned with heavy coats lined in protective sigils, setting them out like offerings on the long entry bench. "These are washed in mountain spring water," he said. "Elementals should ignore us."

"Should," Tadhg echoed, coming in with an armload of satchels. "But you know how elementals get around misused magic. Everything on his land is probably spitting mad."

Eamon placed a wrapped bundle on the coffee table and peeled back the linen. A set of carved charms—rowan, quartz, copper, bone —gleamed in the candlelight. "Protection. Deflection. One for grounding. One for masking your magical signature." He handed each woman a charm. "Wear them close to the skin."

Jade looped hers over her neck without hesitation. Laurie's fingers trembled as she tied hers around her wrist. Skye pressed hers to her chest for a heartbeat before fastening it.

"What about you?" she asked.

He pointed to his chest. "Already handled."

Fíona added a set of small glass vials, each swirling with faint color. "Just in case. Don't drink more than one."

"Ever," Cormac muttered.

Tadhg tossed Jade a compact flashlight, brandishing his own. "Not magical, but bright enough to blind a troll."

Findlay handed Skye a small leather pouch. The familiar weight settled in her palm—a blend of salt, crushed basil, and iron flakes. "For wards," he said quietly.

Skye nodded, throat tight. "Thank you."

The mudroom buzzed as boots thumped, coats swung on shoulders, buckles fastened.

John zipped up his coat, following, but Finlay stopped him. "We're combat trained. Eamon and I were in special forces. You?"

John's mouth worked.

Finlay pointed to the posse. "These three have been touched by magic. We will protect them with our lives."

John stared into Finlay's eyes, then nodded.

As Skye zipped her coat, Cormac touched her shoulder. "You bring her back, lass."

"We will," Skye said. "All of us."

The last pieces of gear were distributed. The Yarrows formed a loose line near the door. Jade squeezed Skye's hand once, grounding her. Laurie gave a firm nod—equal parts fear and determination.

"Let's go," Skye said.

And the Yarrow clan opened the door to the freezing night. At the last minute, Rosa ran after them.

CHAPTER
TWENTY

Dana pulled off the black hood the men had thrust over her head as she pushed herself upright from the stone floor, but only darkness greeted her eyes. No sconces, no glow, not even the faintest outline. A stone room, underground.

Sealed.

Her harsh pants the only sound.

Then somewhere in the dark, something shifted—cloth on stone, the soft scrape of movement.

A voice, rough and ragged, whispered: "Who's there?"

Dana's breath caught.

"Salazar?" she whispered back.

A beat of stunned silence.

"Dana Preston?" His voice shook with disbelief.

"How do you know my name?"

"What in God's name are you doing down here?"

"Following you." Dana let out a humorless laugh. I thought you were working with Vale."

"Me?" His voice lifted in surprise. "No—he's gone too far this time."

Dana crawled toward the voice, her palms brushing cold stone. "Are you hurt?"

"No. Just... shaken." His breath hitched.

Dana's fingers found his sleeve. He was sitting upright, back against the wall. "Where are we?" she asked.

"Underground," he murmured. "One of his hidden structures. I discovered it months ago. He called it a research hall." His voice dropped to a rasp. "It's a temple. Built for his dark rituals."

"So, he's not an antiquities dealer. Or an artifact thief."

Salazar shifted. "No, Adrian Vale has the world fooled. At least most of it. He is a highly trained, quite skilled sorcerer. And now he has Anuun."

Dana's skin prickled. "The skull? The statues? That strange aisle—"

"Yes," he whispered. "He's preparing something. Something dangerous."

The air hummed faintly now, low and resonant, as if the statues remembered her trespass. Dana shivered.

Salazar leaned close. "If he finishes this ritual—"

A distant thud cut him off. Heavy. Metallic. Then a second. Echoing through the floor, through the walls, through the very bones of the place.

Dana's breath caught. "What is that?"

Salazar's voice trembled. "He's opening the hall. The temple doors."

A low vibration rolled beneath them like a living thing.

Above their heads, muffled but unmistakably human, a man began chanting. Deep. Rhythmic. Reverent. The cadence was slow at first—words Dana couldn't understand—but unmistakably ceremonial. Each syllable reverberated through the walls, crawling down her spine.

"That's Vale," Salazar whispered. "He's starting the invocation."

Dana pressed her palm flat to the cold stone. The vibration intensified, as if the entire chamber inhaled with the chant. Warm currents moved through the air—unnatural in the freezing room—swirling like unseen fingers brushing her hair back.

The floor seemed to pulse.

Salazar grabbed her wrist. "When Anuun is invoked, it creates a bridge—he will use the Harmonic Conductor Disk to bring the Guide through. If he succeeds…"

"Anuun will be corrupted." Dana shook her head, trying to steady herself.

"We have to save the Pure One." Salazar sounded desperate.

Dana and Salazar moved to the door, pushing against it, but it held fast. They felt around the walls of their cell, fingers searching for any weakness, any way out.

Suddenly, a new voice called out from above. "Magus, may we enter?"

"Fairfax," Salazar spit out.

"Reginald Fairfax? His cousin?"

"He's brought the rest of Vale's sycophants."

SNOW WHISPERED through the trees as Skye, Jade, Laurie with Rosa, and the Yarrow men followed the narrow trail down to where the family trucks were parked. Their breath fogged in front of them, boots crunching in the crystalline hush. Far behind them, the lights of the house glimmered through the snowfall—warm, bright, oblivious.

Ahead lay darkness.

Tadhg drove the lead truck, tires gripping through the fresh powder. In the backseat, Skye watched the trees blur past, unease twisting beneath her ribs. Jade sat beside her, scanning the map Maxwell had texted again—now annotated with red circles and lines.

Laurie sat in the middle, staring at the video still frozen on her phone: Dana on her knees, pushing under the fence.

"It's my fault," Laurie murmured. "She went after him because of me."

Skye touched her hand. "She made a choice. And now we make ours."

Rosa licked Laurie's chin. *We couldn't go. We didn't know she'd be captured.*

The truck slowed. Cormac had stopped on the twisty road that curved toward Vale's wooded property. The headlights cut a sharp tunnel through the snow-laden branches.

"This is as far as we drive," Finlay said.

They disembarked into knee-deep snow. The cold bit instantly, sharp as teeth. Skye pulled her hood up, feeling the weight of the charm warm faintly against her skin. She looked back and saw Mateo, half-hidden behind the truck, pull his shirt over his head. He bent to pull off the rest of his clothes.

"I'm shifting. I can follow her scent." He grinned. "Plus, I'll be warm." He shimmered and seemed to melt away.

A massive, slate-furred wolf, the kind of creature whispered about in old forest lore, stepped around the truck. His coat was a deep storm-gray dappled with streaks of silver, as if moonlight itself threaded through his fur. His eyes, a piercing, molten gold, burned like twin embers.

The wolf led the way down the unplowed road and trotted along the fence line of Vale's property, the others following in the trail he made. He paused. And there, half-buried under fresh snow, was the gap Dana had crawled through. Mateo ducked under the fence and ran into the trees away from the main house. One by one, the human group scooted under. Once the last person brushed the snow off his jacket, they followed the narrow trail the wolf had made, snow falling heavier now.

Laurie picked Rosa up and stuffed her in the front of her jacket. *This snow is too deep for you.*

Between the trees, strange shadows moved—the restless flicker of elementals drifting near the property line, disturbed by Vale's

CRYSTALS, CROOKS, AND CHAOS

magic. One dark shape dipped low near the ground, hissing before vanishing in a burst of frost.

Laurie shivered violently. "I hate this place."

Rosa let out a low growl.

"You're not alone," Jade murmured.

Tadhg pushed to the front of the group. "Hold up. Let me see if I can talk to this snow."

Laurie watched as Tadhg spread his hands out and made a sweeping gesture. Then raised them to the sky and pushed them back toward the earth. She realized with a start he was creating a quick sacred circle. He held his palms up and began to whisper, his tone beseeching.

After a minute, he reversed his gestures and murmured, "The circle is open." He nodded to the group. "Let's go."

Laurie didn't notice any appreciable let down in the snow fall. Until she took a few steps and it changed to light flurries.

"Thank you," she heard Tadhg whisper. Then in a louder voice, "We've got about two hours before it starts in earnest again."

They moved through the woods as silently as they could, Rosa grumbling that Ashe and Taran didn't make this kind of noise. Soon a low, rectangular building covered in snow appeared among the trees.

Finlay lifted his head. "Skye. Something's moving in there. The energy's wrong."

Jade pulled out her flashlight. Skye laid a hand on her wrist. "Not yet. We don't want to be seen."

The snow on the path that led to the front of the chapel was trampled with many footprints. The sound of chanting reached them.

"They've already started," Laurie said.

Skye took a breath. Cold air burned down her throat. Her heart steadied. "Okay," she whispered. "Let's go get Dana."

The Yarrows moved into formation, flurries swirling around them like ghost-lights. Snow muffled every sound as Skye, Jade,

Laurie, Mateo, and the Yarrow men made their way through the trees onto the trampled path. Laurie put Rosa down and she trotted beside her, tail low, ears high and alert. The chapel sat serene and idyllic, postcard perfect for Christmas Eve, but as they got closer, Skye felt it.

A pulse. A thrum. A wrongness. Like a heartbeat that wasn't human. Even the air thickened—heavier, charged, vibrating with ritual energy.

Jade shivered. "That's not good."

"Understatement," Laurie whispered. Rosa pressed against her leg, growling low in her throat.

Tadhg held up a hand. "Listen."

A chant drifted through the trees—low voices in guttural harmony, each phrase snapping like flint against stone. Even without magic, it made the skin crawl.

Finlay pointed. "There."

A faint glow seeped from the high slit windows—too steady for firelight, too cold for electric.

Eamon whispered, "Energy in there is... twisting."

Tadhg nodded tightly. "Feels like a ritual built on the bones of something older."

"Older and furious," Skye murmured.

Jade held up her hands, palms toward the chapel. "He's got wards, but they're sloppy. He's rushing whatever he's doing."

Another pulse rolled through them—heavier this time. Skye staggered a step before Jade steadied her.

Then—Anuun.

The sense of him shivered along her senses, like a familiar voice calling from behind a closed door. Warm. Wise. Waiting.

"Skye," Jade whispered urgently, "you with me?"

"I think we've found him," Skye said.

"The skull?" Laurie asked.

"We have to go in. Now," Skye said. The energy of the ritual swirled around her.

Finlay took the lead, moving silently along the wall until he found a narrow maintenance door. Eamon whispered a spell of unbinding. The lock gave a soft metallic sigh.

Inside, the corridor sloped downward, carved stone replacing metal walls. The air thickened further—stale, sacred, humming with ritual tension.

They moved in silence.

At the corridor's end, a massive archway opened onto a cavernous hall: towering statues flanking a central aisle—stone gods with glittering eyes, ancient guardians whose presence made the air press tight against the skin. Their carved faces seemed to watch...or wait.

But it was the dais at the end of the hall that stole every breath.

Vale.

He stood draped in ceremonial robes, deep crimson trimmed in metallic sigils that pulsed faintly with power. A ring of robed acolytes surrounded him, chanting in a harsh, rhythmic cadence that vibrated through the floor and into the bones.

And at the heart of their circle—elevated on its obsidian pedestal—Anuun.

The crystal skull glowed, fractured light shimmering beneath its surface like trapped lightning.

But something else dominated the space.

In front of Vale, hovering just above the stone tiles, was a disk—metallic, ancient, etched in spiraling runes that seemed to rearrange themselves as Skye watched.

The Harmonic Conductor Disk.

The disk thrummed with layered tones, a chord that wasn't a sound so much as a *pressure,* building in slow, relentless waves. Each pulse bent the air, warping the candle flames, twisting the shadows behind the statues.

Jade inhaled sharply. "It's what Maxwell predicted. He's not just calling on the skull. He's using the disk as a frequency anchor."

Laurie clutched Rosa instinctively. "I...I can feel it. Something pushing."

The little dog struggled out of her arms and ducked behind one of the statues. *Mateo* was all she said. Laurie attention snapped back to Vale.

Skye's hand flew to her chest, steadying the wild flutter in her ribcage. The air ahead shimmered—no, stretched, as if reality itself were thinning. A faint circular distortion hovered behind the pedestal, like heat haze but darker... deeper...wrong.

Tadhg whispered, "Gods preserve us. He's opening a portal."

The tones intensified, layering over the chanting, creating an agonizing, discordant sound that made the statues tremble. Dust sifted from their stone shoulders.

The Conductor Disk spun slowly, runes brightening with every rotation. A low moan of wind rose from nowhere, pulling inward toward the center of the circle—toward the forming breach.

Eamon stepped back involuntarily. "Something's pushing from the other side."

Laurie's breath fogged sharply. "I can hear—it's like...like something wants to come through."

Jade reached for Skye's hand, squeezing tight. "We need to get Anuun out before Vale finishes this."

But Skye couldn't look away.

Because in that moment, through the distortion, through the bending air and warping shadows—a shape pressed against the inner surface of the forming portal. Indistinct. Humanoid. But far too tall, its proportions off, its outline shimmering like a being made of flame and bones.

The entity pushed harder.

The Harmonic Conductor Disk shrieked a new chord, violent and dissonant, vibrating the very stones beneath their feet.

Vale lifted his hands triumphantly. "The Guide comes! Anuun opens the way!"

Skye felt Anuun's light flare—like a desperate warning. And the wrongness surged like a wave through the hall.

The portal's surface bowed inward, the being pressing harder, its blazing silhouette flickering in and out of existence like a glitch in reality. The harmonic tones built to a vibrating, metallic wail.

Skye's breath caught. Her fingertips tingled. Her vision blurred at the edges—and then snapped sharply into focus.

Anuun's light brightened, cascading in prismatic shards across the pedestal. Warm. Urgent.

Skye.

The whisper wasn't sound. It bloomed inside her mind like a burst of golden fire. She staggered a step forward before Jade clamped a hand on her arm.

"Skye—wait—"

But Skye couldn't tear her gaze away. The skull's inner fractures glowed brighter with every pulse from the Harmonic Conductor Disk, as if Anuun were fighting the pull of the ritual.

You must stop him...before the threshold breaks...

Skye swallowed, dizzy from the force of it. "Anuun's reaching for me," she murmured. "He needs us to stop this."

Laurie grabbed her other arm. "Then we get him out—now—before that thing comes through!"

Another pulse of wrongness washed over them—thick as tar, scraping at the edges of their minds. The Yarrow men flinched.

And then Vale's voice cracked through the hall: "Who speaks?"

Vale's head snapped toward the archway. His eyes locked on Skye—wide, wild, shining with the manic fervor of a zealot at the height of revelation.

"You!" His voice deepened unnaturally, echoing against the stone. "How dare you interrupt this sacred rite!"

He lifted one shaking hand and jabbed a finger toward her. "Seize her!"

Two robed men broke from the circle immediately, robes billowing as they sprinted up the central aisle. Their faces were pale, pupils blown wide from the ritual's energy.

Skye stumbled back. Jade caught her. Tadhg and Findlay barreled forward to intercept, but the magic in the room fought them—air thickening, slowing their steps, tugging at their limbs like invisible vines.

The Harmonic Conductor Disk emitted a keening vibrato, warping the air around it.

Vale snarled, voice booming, "Now I understand. She is the one the Anuun recognizes—and she is the key to the portal!"

Jade's eyes widened. "Skye—he needs *you* to open it!"

Skye blanched. "Over my dead body."

The two robed enforcers lunged—but before they could reach her, the portal behind the pedestal convulsed. The circular distortion rippled violently, sucking air toward it in a gale-force pull. The statues lining the hall vibrated, their carved arms quivering as if straining against stone.

A crackling sound—like splitting ice—reverberated through the chamber. The being behind the veil pushed harder. Its elongated hand, made of shimmering red-white energy, pressed hard, deforming the membrane of reality like a fingertip stretching rubber.

No. Anuun's voice cut through Skye's mind like a blade of light. *It is not the Guide—it is not who he thinks.*

That much seemed obvious to the Yarrow clan.

The Harmonic Conductor Disk spun faster, runes blazing, lines of power whipping around it like electrical tendrils. Sparks jumped between the disk and the portal, fusing the energies together.

A shockwave burst outward.

Laurie screamed as the force threw her back against the archway.

Jade staggered and clung to Skye.

Tadhg slammed both hands against the floor, anchoring himself with magic to resist the pull.

Finlay shouted, "He's losing control!"

Eamon yelled over the wailing disk, "If that portal tears fully—whatever that thing is—it's coming through!"

The robed enforcers covering their heads retreated in fear.

Even Vale faltered, stumbling backward, eyes flicking between the disk and the buckling portal.

"No—no—this isn't right—the frequency is off—" His voice cracked into panic. "The guide should have appeared by now!"

The portal shuddered, its surface fracturing like a mirror struck by a hammer.

Skye, heart pounding, grabbed Jade's hand. Jade squeezed back fiercely.

Anuun's inner light flared again—*Take me out of the circle. Break the link.*

The portal screamed—the force like a psychic howl tearing at their minds—and the being pushed again, its distorted form forcing through the cracking veil.

"Go now," Jade shouted.

Skye ran for the pedestal—just as Vale screamed, "Stop her!"

CHAPTER
TWENTY-ONE

The ceiling in Dana and Salazar's cell shook, plaster falling to the floor.

"What is going on?" Dana spread the hood over her head trying to protect herself.

"He's activated the disk," Salazar spit out.

Above them, the chanting grew louder, layering into a dissonant harmony that made Dana's teeth ache. She could only imagine how Anuun suffered after the glorious song he'd been listening to.

She pressed her ear to the door of their cell. Her stomach dropped. Footsteps directly outside the chamber. Several pairs. Moving in sync, like guards shifting into position.

And then—

A scream. Distant, muffled, but unmistakable.

Dana jerked upright. "Who was that?"

Vale's voice, magically amplified, rolled through the temple—smooth, ritualistic, brimming with triumph. "Tonight, the veil opens," he intoned. "Tonight, Anuun speaks."

Dana couldn't believe her ears. Anuun didn't need any help to speak. Did this man think he was making the skull talk?

Salazar's grip tightened painfully around Dana's hand. "We have to get out," he whispered. "Now."

Dana's heart pounded. Outside, the chanting surged.

Inside, the lock on their door clicked again.

Someone—or something—was coming.

The heavy lock on Dana and Salazar's cell door scraped again—this time not with the cold, mechanical finality of a guard closing them in, but with a swift, decisive click.

The door swung open.

Dana squinted into the harsh fluorescent light.

A man stood in the doorway.

A very naked man.

Dana blinked. She'd seen him before. Somewhere. Red Fox Farm. "Mateo?"

He gave an apologetic wince. "Sorry. I left my clothes in the car. I'm going to shift back in a second."

Salazar made a strangled noise. "Dear God."

Mateo stepped in and pulled the door shut. "We don't have time. Skye and the others are inside the ritual hall. Vale saw them."

Dana gasped. "Skye—no. We have to get to them."

The walls of the cell groaned, stones shifting.

"We have to go now." Mateo took a step back, braced himself, and said, "Okay. Don't freak out."

Dana opened her mouth to ask why—but Mateo's body turned to gel, his features melting away. Then it reshaped, fur rippling over muscle in a fluid, impossible wave. In less than two heartbeats, a massive wolf stood in the small chamber—silver-furred, eyes bright with intelligence, power rolling off him like heat.

Dana stumbled back, breath trapped in her lungs. "Holy—"

"Well," Salazar whispered, staring openly, "that's not something you see every day."

The wolf huffed, clearly impatient.

Salazar opened the cell door and Rosa darted in, barking sharply

—three times—then trotted a few steps down the hall. She paused, looked back, barked again.

Dana stared at her. "Are you—are you going to turn into something too?"

Rosa froze. Then she gave Dana the flattest, most exasperated *dog* look Dana had ever seen.

The wolf snorted.

Salazar murmured, "I think that's a no."

Rosa barked again—urgently this time—and spun toward the hall.

Dana swallowed, "Okay, we're coming. Geez."

Dana and Salazar hurried down the narrow stone corridor, Rosa trotting ahead with sharp, purposeful barks. Mateo—the wolf—moved like a shadow beside them, muscles rippling beneath his thick silver fur. He glanced back to be sure they kept up.

The chanting above had broken into chaos—shouts, frantic footsteps, the clatter of something heavy falling. The air vibrated with a strange, unstable energy.

Rosa barked once, sharply, then sprinted up a narrow flight of stairs.

Dana swallowed hard and followed. At the top was an alcove overlooking the ritual hall. Dana pressed herself to the stone railing and gasped.

Below them—

Skye was held by two robed magicians, her arms pinned as she fought. Her charm necklace glowed so brightly it hurt to look at. Jade was struggling with another attacker across the room. Laurie tried to push toward Skye, but Fairfax blocked her. The Yarrow men fought from the edges of the circle, using both fists and streams of magic to keep Vale's followers off-balance.

Vale stood in the center, chest heaving, robes disheveled, one hand gripping **a** gun—pointed directly at Skye's heart.

"Do you fools understand nothing?" he roared. "This ritual

cannot be interrupted! You have no idea what you're meddling with!"

Anuun pulsed on the pedestal, a stream light shooting out toward Skye.

Salazar inhaled sharply. "Oh god—he's armed. Skye—she's—"

Dana's breath froze.

The gun cocked.

The wolf's ears pricked forward. And then he *flew*.

A flash of silver shot past Dana so fast she didn't register movement—just explosive action. The wolf vaulted over the railing, a streak of fur and fury, landing on Vale with bone-jarring force.

Vale screamed as he crashed onto the stone floor. The gun skittered across the hall, spinning under a statue's outstretched foot.

The wolf snarled—deep, primal, teeth bared inches from Vale's throat.

The magicians holding Skye faltered in shock. The rift above was folding in on itself. An unearthly scream sounded from beyond the membrane.

That was all she needed. Skye shoved backward, slammed her heel into one man's knee, and jabbed an elbow into the other's jaw. Jade sprinted across the hall and tackled the first robed man trying to recover.

Finlay and Eamon surged forward, binding two more sycophants with the cords torn from their ceremonial robes—twisted rope dyed black and silver, embroidered by rank. Tadhg grabbed another, twisting his arm behind his back while Rosa nipped sharply at his ankles.

Laurie snatched up the gun and kicked Vale's nearest follower in the ribs. "Nobody move!"

The chanting was gone. The portal snapped shut. Only ragged breathing, scuffling feet, and Vale's wounded wheezing filled the air.

Dana and Salazar ran down the narrow steps and burst into the hall.

Skye looked up, relief flooding her features. "Dana!"

Dana ran to her and threw her arms around her. Jade joined them, arms encircling both. Skye trembled for a split second, then steadied.

Rosa barked triumphantly.

Salazar exhaled slowly, shaky with adrenaline. "Thank every god listening."

Mateo paced beside Vale, low growls rumbling in his chest, daring him to twitch.

Finlay tugged one bound sycophant upright. "That's the last of them."

Eamon finished tying Vale's wrists with a robe cord and hauled him roughly to his feet. Vale's face twisted with livid fury.

"You idiots!" he spat. "You have no idea what you've stopped. The guide was coming. Anuun was ready. You have doomed—"

Rosa barked sharply. *Shut it.*

Laurie smirked. "Yeah, what she said."

"That wasn't Anuun's guide," Salazar said, his voice shaking. "You almost ruined the last ancient master skull."

Skye walked to the pedestal, reverent and certain. Anuun glimmered softly as she touched the skull, lifting him gently into her arms.

Warmth spread through the hall—relief, gratitude, a soft pulse of recognition.

"Let's go," Skye said. "This place feels like it's collapsing."

Indeed, the energy around them was fraying. Statues flickered with shifting shadows. The air trembled.

Finlay jerked Vale forward. "Move."

They herded Vale and his robed followers out, leaving the fractured ritual circle behind. Mateo shifted back to human form the moment they reached the corridor—Salazar thrust his outer coat at him without looking.

"Thank you," Mateo muttered, scrambling into it.

The night hit them in a blast of frigid air as they emerged from the temple. Snow fell in thick sheets now—heavy, swirling, relentless.

Skye clutched Anuun under her coat, protecting him from the cold. The skull's inner light glowed softly against her chest.

Mateo and the Yarrow men dragged the bound magicians into Vale's mansion. "What should we do with them?"

Salazar stood in front of the disheveled, furious men. "Well, we can't exactly call the police. There's no law against unleashing a demonic being into a crystal skull, no matter how big a cosmic crime it is."

"I'm glad you realize at least that much. You've ruined everything." Vale looked at Fairfax whose left eye was swelling shut. "We'll just have to rebuild."

Tadgh stepped forward. "If you ever try to mess with us again—if you ever touch a hair on any of my families' head, come on our land or into one of our businesses—if you even think of taking this crystal again—" he shook his head, leaving the threat unspoken.

The Yarrow men untied the magicians and slammed the door of the mansion behind them. They trudged through the snow toward the trucks, breath fogging in the cold air, the adrenaline finally ebbing into bone-deep exhaustion. No one spoke.

Then—a sharp crack split the night.

Everyone froze.

Skye turned first.

Another crack followed—louder, deeper—like a massive beam snapping under impossible strain. Rosa bristled. Mateo shifted his stance, senses flaring.

A low groan rose from behind them, the sound of wood twisting against itself. Snow sifted from the pines as the earth gave a subtle shudder.

Jade whispered, "Oh... wow."

They watched as the hidden building—once solid timber and dark shingles—buckled inward. The central frame collapsed with a roar, walls folding as if a giant hand had crushed the structure from above. Lantern glass burst in showers of sparks. Support beams snapped, dropping in jagged silhouettes against the snow.

Within seconds, the entire building imploded in on itself. A final, thunderous crash shook the clearing.

And then—silence.

Where the temple had stood only moments before, there was nothing but a heap of smoldering wood and drifting ash. Snowflakes spiraled down, hissing softly as they touched the warm debris.

Laurie swallowed. "It's...gone."

Skye tightened her grip on Anuun beneath her coat. His light pulsed once—low and relieved, like an exhale.

"Good," she murmured. "Let it stay gone."

No one argued.

Together, they turned back toward the trucks, snow crunching underfoot as the night closed quietly around them.

The wind picked up.

Hard.

"What is *with* this storm?" Dana shouted over the gust.

"Magical backlash," Tadgh answered. "I asked it to stop, which is unnatural. Now the full force it held back for me is coming through."

By the time they reached the trucks, the snowfall had become blinding—thick flakes whipping sideways, stinging faces and hands.

Everyone piled in quickly, breath fogging the windows. The Yarrow trucks rumbled to life, headlights carving through the white-out. As they drove away, the mansion vanished behind them— swallowed by darkness and a blizzard that felt almost supernatural.

Skye looked down at Anuun glowing faintly in her lap. "We've got you," she whispered. "You're safe now."

The skull seemed to close his eyes and sleep.

Snow thickened on the road, bogging down their progress while Seattle drivers wobbled between panic and paralysis. Some had surrendered entirely, hazards blinking as they waited out the storm on the side of the road. Others skidded into fenders and bumpers, creating glittering, snow-dusted pileups. The rest crawled forward at a glacial five miles per hour.

The snow softened as they neared Duvall, tapering to a gentle dusting that clung to the shoulders of pines and fence posts. When the wheels crunched into the gravel at Red Fox Farm, the storm simply let go. Above them, a wide, clear sky opened, and single bright star hovered bright and still, as if blessing the long winter night.

CHAPTER
TWENTY-TWO

They piled out of the car and plowed through the snow, Finlay, Tadgh, and Eamon going ahead and forming a passage. Laurie, Dana and Jade surrounded Skye as she carried Anuun wrapped in her arms like a new-born infant. Not exactly the baby the world was welcoming tonight, but a beam of light all the same.

Salazar hung back.

"Wait," Dana whispered and turned to him. "Come with us."

"You sure?" he asked.

"You helped us," Skye said. "Please come inside so my family can thank you."

He followed behind them, his tweed coat fluttering in the breeze like some professorial shepherd.

Ashe and Taran greeted Rosa halfway to the house, sniffing her all over. Laurie could hear Rosa telling the story of their adventure as they escorted her inside.

"Mom!" Hoa shouted, running to Dana who wrapped her arms around the young teen. Minh followed, dropping his cool long enough to encircle them both in a huge hug.

He pulled back and studied her face in the porch light. "Are you hurt? We thought...you've got to stop scaring us."

"I'm fine." Dana pushed his hair back from his eyes and smiling.

Maxwell stood on the porch, pretending nonchalance. "So, you stopped the evil wizard, I see."

Fíona and Cormac pushed past him, running to Skye. "Are you all right? We felt—I can't even explain what we felt," Fíona said, eyes wide.

Cormac reared back. "You," he said to Salazar.

Dana put her hand on his arm. "He's on our side."

"He helped in the big fight," Skye said.

"Fight?" Cormac's eyes took on a fierce look.

"We're fine," Jade patted her father-in-law's shoulder.

John was right on their heels. He grabbed Laurie and twirled her around. "I was so worried. I should have gone with you."

"Our warriors protected us," Laurie said.

"They were amazing," Skye said.

"You fought pretty good yourselves," Finlay shouted from the porch.

Siobhán and Brenna stood next to the three warriors, arms wrapped around themselves against the cold.

"Into the house with ye," Grandmother Moira ordered, standing in the doorway. "Yer lettin' all the heat out. We'll have to burn a whole forest to get warm again."

Skye climbed the steps surrounded by a swarm of people.

"In with ye now. I see ye brought that skull with ye." Grandmother Moira still seemed to have her doubts.

"Let's go into the living room. We can all have a look at it," Fíona said.

The moment they stepped back into the big Yarrow house, the warmth wrapped around them like an embrace. The group crowded in, the rest of the clan pushing together to give them room to sit. Fíona picked up a tray of fudge and gingerbread men to clear space on the long coffee table, and Skye set Anuun down.

He sat quiet for a few seconds, then seemed to wake slowly from his nap as the clan gathered around, oohing and aahing.

"Wow, it's pretty."

"Look at the rainbows."

"It's a little scary."

"You'll like him once he lights up," Sorcha reassured the younger ones.

The skull brightened and the children sent up a gasp of wonder.

The chaos from earlier had settled into a soft, joyful hum. Carols drifted from the old speakers—sweet, familiar, and comforting—and the towering Douglas fir sparkled as if delighted they'd finally returned.

Presents still sat under the branches, wrapped and waiting, exactly as they'd been left when everyone had bolted toward the crisis. Now, the family gathered again—this time calmer, glowing with relief—and began handing them out.

Paper tore. Ribbons fluttered. Bright laughter rose as boxes opened and treasures were revealed: knitted scarves in jewel tones, carved wooden toys, jars of Fíona's prized blackberry jam, books, puzzles, and handcrafted charms meant to guard and guide.

Anuun had moved to the mantle where he sat safely casting a soft, shimmering glow across the room. Clan members wandered by, pausing in quiet wonder as if greeting an honored guest. His rainbow glints sparkled over cheeks flushed with warmth and gratitude.

"Food!" Siobhán called from the kitchen doorway, her hands on her hips and a no-nonsense glint in her eye. "Before it goes cold!"

Grandmother Brigid joined her with a wooden spoon raised like a conductor's wand. "Come on, mo chroí. The table's groaning."

And it was. The long kitchen table nearly bowed beneath the feast, golden turkey slices steaming beside bowls of buttery mashed potatoes, roasted root vegetables glazed with herbs and honey, warm soda bread tucked in cloth, patters of smoked salmon, and a tureen of rich cullen skink that perfumed the air. Spices, savory and sweet, mixed with the scent of pine and candlewax, creating a holiday alchemy all its own.

"What's that?" John asked, pointing at the tureen.

"I think it's a Scottish fish chowder," Laurie said.

"You're right," Siobhán whispered beside them.

The two turned and laughed, their cheeks flushing. "Thanks for the tip," Laurie said.

People loaded plates, then drifted back to the living room to eat by the fire. Two of the older uncles quietly switched the TV to a live airing of midnight mass from St. Patrick's Cathedral in New York City. A hush fell over that corner of the room—some watching reverently, others simply comforted by the familiar pageantry.

The younger children tried valiantly to stay awake, but warm food and safe arms won out. They curled like kittens, heads on parents' laps, blankets drawn up to chins, soft snores blending with the choir on the screen.

The dogs were rewarded for their service with enormous knucklebones. Ashe dragged hers to a plush bed near the hearth. Taran pranced proudly with his before flopping onto a pillow pile. Even Rosa accepted her treat with an air of well-earned dignity, settling beside Laurie with tail thumping.

Gandalf, the old cat, had made the journey up from Skye and Jade's place earlier in the evening. He eased himself onto the luxurious cat bed set before the fire as if it were a throne prepared expressly for him. He purred once—deep, approving—and promptly fell asleep.

Laughter mingled with the crackling logs. Someone clinked a mug. Someone else sighed with contentment. The house glowed with that peculiar magic that only comes after danger has passed and loved ones are safe again.

Skye sat close to Jade, their shoulders touching, Anuun's soft light flickering over their faces. Laurie fed sleepy Rosa bits of turkey. Dana leaned against the arm of the couch, watching her children—

Minh absorbed in a new book, Hoa braiding a bracelet from yarn Aunt Nia had gifted her.

Even Salazar, patched up and exhausted, managed a smile as he accepted a cup of spiced cider.

His phone buzzed.

He checked the screen. *Celeste.*

He stepped into the quieter hall and answered, voice soft. "Salazar here."

"Seraphina says the Pure One has been rescued," Celeste said, sounding relieved and a touch breathless, as if she too had been holding vigil.

A smile pulled at Salazar's mouth. He glanced into the glowing living room, at Skye laughing with Jade, at Anuun gleaming warmly on the mantle. "Yes. He's safe. He's in very good hands...and they said I can visit him." Emotion thickened his voice for a moment.

"Think I could..." Celeste paused.

Salazar knew what she was asking but hesitant to say. "You could probably come see Anuun. Just ask Skye."

"You think?" Celeste sounded like a delighted kid.

"I do." Salazar smiled, knowing how much this meant to her. "Thank you for checking in."

"Of course," Celeste murmured. "Merry Christmas, Victor."

He exhaled, the warmth of the house spreading through him. "Merry Christmas, Celeste."

He hung up and rejoined the others—drawn back into the glow, the laughter, the firelight, and the soft winter star shining through the windows.

Skye slipped away from the chatter for a moment, wandering to the window where the snowfall had quieted. Outside, Red Fox Farm lay blanketed in moonlit silver, the pines dusted white, the fields stretching peaceful and untouched. The bright star overhead shimmered like it was keeping watch—over the land, over the family she loved, over the fragile boundary between their world and the unseen. The long night had ended.

She pressed a hand to her heart, feeling Anuun's calming presence pulsing faintly across the room. He wasn't just an artifact or a relic of some forgotten age. He was...a promise. A reminder that wisdom endured, even when darkness pressed close.

Behind her, Jade laughed softly at something Laurie said. Dana murmured to Minh as he showed her a book. Rosa barked happily in her sleep. Gandalf snored like a tiny chainsaw. It was all wonderfully ordinary. Beautifully alive. And so very precious.

Skye let her eyes close for a heartbeat, gratitude flooding through her. For her family. For her friends. For second chances. For the kind of love that survived storms—and sometimes carried her through them.

When she turned back to the room, Jade met her gaze with a soft smile that said *I see you.*

Skye breathed in the warmth, the music, the glow.

"Yeah," she whispered to herself. "We're going to be just fine."

And with that, she went back to join the people who made the long night worth surviving.

THANKS FOR READING CRYSTALS, *Crooks, and Chaos.* I hope you enjoyed reading it as much as I enjoyed writing it. I wrote all three of these books in a year and a half, so I'm going to take some time to breathe and work on other projects. I love the posse and Rosa (my Egyptologist's favorite character), so I will write more. For those who want to return to the Emerald City, subscribe to my newsletter here or go to www.theresalcrater.com.

OR Claim your copy of "The Antique Shop"and sign up. Not spamy and you can cancel any time.

~

IF YOU LOVED the mid-life magic of the Emerald City books, discover the Witch of Spirit Springs series. *The Crone and the Stolen Orb* ~ A magical orb. A cranky witch. A job from the High Fae she never asked for. Click here to check it out.

~

THANK YOU FOR READING CRYSTALS, *Crooks, and Chaos*. Your honest review will help future readers decide if they want to take a chance on a new-to-them author. Just click here to leave a review.

. . .

ACKNOWLEDGMENTS

I am very grateful to all my readers. You make it possible. A special shout out to my advanced readers for their eagle eyes and helpful suggestions.

I appreciate my coaches at Author Ad School for guiding me through the maze of the writing business.

Thank you double to Karri Klawiter, my super talented cover designer, who doesn't even yell at me for last minute changes.

Special thanks to Stephen Mehler, who is my constant companion at home and abroad. And Cleopatra Iset, who brings me mice and other gifts.

About the Author

Theresa Crater is a bestselling author of award-winning supernatural suspense, contemporary fantasy, and paranormal mystery. Based in the foothills of Colorado, she travels extensively to write fantasy fiction exploring world mythologies, sacred sites, and the universal search for spiritual and human connection.

She has published over thirty works of fiction. She is the author of the Spirit Springs series, the Emerald City Mysteries, the Power Places series, Mystic Assassin thrillers, and other works.

Also By

Breached: A Mystic Assassin Novella

Louise Ryder

God in a Box

School of Hard Knocks